THE HORSE'S ARSE

or

THE SHED OF REVELATION

Laura Gascoigne

Clink
Street

Published by Clink Street Publishing 2017

Copyright © 2017

First edition.

ISBN: 978-1-911110-87-3 PAPERBACK
978-1-911110-88-0 EBOOK

To the Unknown Artist

Chapter I

"Left a little... Up a little. Turn your head to the window so the light falls on your nose – that's it – and dream. Dream of your first lover... where is he now? Perfect. 'My old flame, I can't even think of his name...' Now bunch your hair and hold it over your ear – so – and draw the comb across *con amore*, like you're playing the cello."

Music, that's what was needed. Dvořák. Would Degas have listened to Dvořák? Dvořák was Czech and Degas was French, and anyway they didn't have records then. He must have painted in silence.

Pat considered this possibility, rejected it and crossed the studio to find the cello concerto. He handled the 1970s Philips record player *con amore*. Top of the range machine, a bargain buy. And look, the shade of orange matched his socks.

As the recording scratched into life, a shaft of dusty spring sunlight broke through the window and transfigured the middle-aged woman on the couch, heightening the white of her skin against the red of her hair and setting the yellow throw beneath her aglow. Pity about the tongue and groove behind. He'd have to bodge the Chinese wallpaper.

Killer combo, cerulean and cadmium yellow. He rattled around in his box of pastels and picked out a blue one. A few deft strokes of cerulean over cobalt, some buds of lemon

1

yellow, a tracery of burnt sienna and bang! The tongue and groove was fin de siècle Chinoiserie.

Pat consulted the open book on the painting table. Hmmm. He'd have preferred the pose of the D'Orsay picture with the model on the floor completely nude, one leg tucked in, the other bent in front and both arms raised above the shoulder, brushing the hair up from the nape of the neck. But that was a bit athletic for Irene.

Good old Irene. Must have been a beauty, and still moved her old bones like a cat. There was something naturally statuesque about her. She didn't perch like an amateur, she *sat*. And the pose of the Hermitage picture came out sexier if approached from the left, exposing both breasts and the model's mouth.

Irene had a good mouth. He touched it in with Indian red. It yawned.

"Time for a break, I'll put the kettle on," said Pat, returning the Indian red to the box with special care.

Nice of Martin to get him Unison pastels. Quality gear, soft on the hands as talc and saturated in pigment. Hand-rolled between the thighs of Northumbrian maidens, with none of the usual binder muck thrown in. Not much different, he reckoned, from the pastels Degas used. Martin could be surprisingly generous sometimes.

Pat crossed the patch of garden to the kitchen quickly. Since the second hip replacement he'd had a limp, but he always crossed the garden quickly in case Ron next door came out and collared him.

That was the trouble with the 'burbs, your neighbours. Ron was still hopping mad about The Shed despite the fact that it had improved the property. Before it went up he'd never stopped complaining about the tip at the bottom of the garden. So what if Pat hadn't got planning permission? Since when did you need permission to plan? Next thing you knew, you'd need a licence to dream.

Anyway it wasn't any business of Ron's what went on at the bottom of Pat's garden. Some people had fairies, Pat had The

Shed of Revelation and a bloody fine specimen of a shed it was too. Dino had done a fearless construction job, far better than Martin. If Martin had built it water would be coming in. Shame that someone as brilliant at building should be so hopeless at painting. Ah well, Dino was a 3-D man.

Returning with the mugs of tea, Pat risked a momentary halt in mid-garden to admire The Shed of Rev's front elevation. How Dino had managed to build a double-fronted cabin with a veranda entirely out of skip wood was a miracle. All that was needed for perfection was a rocking chair, but in a rocking chair he'd be a sitting duck for Ron.

He could see Irene standing framed in the left-hand window in her old kimono, holding a cigarette and wearing the exact expression he'd been after. That was a picture worth painting, but it would have to wait. Funny how many artists painted women from behind looking out of windows and how few thought of doing them from in front.

So many pictures to be painted, and so little time.

On his way back in with the teas, he raised the mugs in a silent toast to the stack of tall canvases propped against the wall to the right of the entrance. "You too my beauties, I haven't forgotten you," he whispered mentally. "You're the real McCoy. But first we must get Degas out of the way."

The money would keep Moira happy, that was the main thing. Not that she ever complained, but that made things worse. If her useless excuse for a second husband would only get off his arse and keep her in the style to which she should have been accustomed it wouldn't be an issue, but every time Pat thought of her scrubbing floors on her hands and knees his heart sank. Beautiful bright Moira working as a cleaner, while he swanned about the place being an artist. Was it self-indulgence? It was what he did. It was a job, unpaid perhaps but a job all the same. Wait until The Seven Seals were opened, then the world would see that Patrick Phelan had not been wasting his time. When the heptatych landed, the world wouldn't know what hit it.

He put the teas down on the table, came up behind Irene and slipped a hand still warm from the mug under her kimono. It squeezed her left breast.

A bit on the soft side, but it still felt good.

Chapter II

Martin Phelan was acting like he owned the place as usual, although it wasn't his house. But it was his handiwork, and he was entitled to feel proprietorial. OK, so the orangery wasn't strictly finished, the landscaped garden was a building site and the lily pond was leaking, but those were all things that could be fixed. Nothing that couldn't be fixed with money, and Orlo had plenty.

The rain was a piece of luck anyway, it would keep people indoors. Not so lucky for the papier mâché sculpture park at ICE, but hey! It was all about entropy. The coke was kicking in and he was feeling positive. He refilled his glass from the catering table, ignoring the bar staff, and went to work the room.

If a bomb went off this evening, Martin was thinking, it would wipe out the whole London contemporary art world plus a sizeable chunk of the global one. On the eve of the first International Contemporary Equity art fair, ICE – a joint venture between auction house RazzellDeVere and *Marquette* magazine – everyone who was anyone was in town and all of them were on Orlo's guest list. For a recession, they were putting on a good show.

Over by the fireplace (yes, a fireplace in an orangery – Orlovsky asked for one and the customer is always right) Martin could see Fay Lacey-Piggott, *Marquette*'s editor-in-chief, in conversation with Nigel Vouvray-Jones, senior director of RazzellDeVere. On the sofa beside them, between two women in white and black dresses – the white mono-chrome minimalist Celeste Buhler and the papier mâché sculptor Heather Manning – sprawled the Dutch painter Dirk Boegemann, his pale blue eyes fastened drunkenly on a voluptuous redhead who was listening with rapt attention to Jason Faith. Jason had won last year's Ars Nova Prize for his *Empty Room*. Martin couldn't imagine what the redhead found so gripping – the guy was on the dumb side of laconic, but he played in a punk band and she looked like a groupie.

On the other side of the room next to the stairs, Mervyn Burke was being monopolised by *Marquette*'s gossip colum-nist and Martin's on-off squeeze Bernice Stock. Martin could see her fat arse blocking the way to the bathroom; he really should have made that passageway bigger. Mervyn had won the previous year's Ars Nova for his *Signature Pieces*. His work was all about leaving traces: he signed things and turned them into money. At ICE he was launching a new series of signed ring stains on conservation quality paper. The only things he didn't sign were banknotes because, he joked, they were signed already. Merv was a laugh.

Martin could see that Bernice was boring him. He watched him move her aside to allow a skinny kid with nipple rings in a torn black singlet slip past to the bathroom with an older man in a pearl grey suit. The skinny kid was Puerto Rican perfor-mance artist Enzo, a specialist in public bloodlettings, and the older man was northern art collector Godfrey Wise. At a party last year Enzo had gone to the toilet and slashed his wrists, and Godfrey obviously didn't want him repeating that here. The incident had got into the tabloids, causing embarrassment. Martin watched them emerge minutes later looking chipper. He smiled as Mervyn moved Bernice aside again to let them pass without any visible interruption to the verbal flow.

Anywhere else this sort of discretion would have been unnecessary, but Orlovsky was a stickler for appearances. Even at home he had his gallery goons on the door. One of them had frisked Martin playfully on the way in and now he was dishing out the same treatment to the art dealer James Duval, who was not looking happy. Never mind, thought Martin, he'll cheer up when he hears about the Degas.

Orlovsky's goons were recruited from the Hoxton gay mafia, and you didn't mess with them. The one by the bar was keeping an eye on Dirk. Martin saw him stiffen as the ascetic figure of Sir Jeremy Gaunt, director of the State Gallery, appeared in the doorway with the flicker of a smile of greeting on his face. A barely perceptible shiver ran through the room.

Security didn't lay a finger on Gaunt, but when video artist Tammy Tinker-Stone crossed the room to film his arrival on her phone, one of the Hoxton heavies took it off her. She shrugged and smirked and came over to where Martin and Duval were standing.

"A fair cop," said Martin.

Tammy had not yet won the Ars Nova and everyone knew she was gagging to. She'd been shortlisted the year before for *Gutted,* her video collage of football managers reacting to missed goals, part of a series exploring the contemporary symbolism of the tragic mask. Now she was collecting smiles on the faces of art world insiders, but it wasn't going well. It lacked the drama and emotional range of the stadium. Recently, though, a new idea had occurred to her, a good one if she could find the right person for it.

"I need an artist," she announced.

"Take your pick," said Duval, waving a dismissive arm around the room.

"Not that kind of artist. A proper artist."

"Proper?" Duval raised a tired eyebrow.

"A painter, I need a painter. Not like Dirk," she jerked her head towards the catering table against which the Dutchman now had the redhead pinned, "an old-fashioned painter. One who uses, you know, colours, an easel, palette, brushes. The works. One who's serious about the whole operation. I want to record the creative act, the image taking shape on the canvas, the whole performance. I want to do painting as performance art. Know anyone?"

"You could ask my Dad," said Martin, "if you don't mind him jumping on you."

"Is he good?"

"What's good?" asked Duval with effete distaste.

"I mean good like a master, like, oh, Degas. Whoever."

Martin glanced at Duval.

"He's good like Degas."

"Can I have his number? Bugger, they've got my phone."

She pulled a pen out of her bag and scribbled the number Martin gave her on the back of her hand.

"By the way," Duval turned to Martin after she'd gone, "my conservatory's leaking."

Chapter III

The halting drip of water into a bucket beat an erratic rhythm to Duval's thoughts as he sat brooding at the desk in his book-lined study. In the gloom of the basement the desk light cast a warm bright circle on a pastel drawing of a bare-breasted redhead sitting on a yellow bedspread combing her hair.

It was unmistakably a Degas, though not a known picture, which could have been an advantage but was actually a problem. Why would an uncatalogued Degas suddenly surface after more a century? The image was evidently a close relation of the oil painting, *Woman Combing her Hair*, in the Hermitage – the same acid yellow bedspread, electric blue wallpaper, nacreous skin and auburn hair. But the pose was different, and the breasts were a little less pert.

Typical of Martin to start at the top; it always had to be big stuff with Martin. He should have warned him to stick to the 20th century, when the materials would be less of a giveaway – though these days who checked? With a modern artist, too, it was more likely that unknown pictures might have fallen through the cracks, especially with an artist of the second league. With a big name like Matisse or Picasso who had been *catalogue-raisonnéed* from here to there, provenance became a major problem.

He picked up an eyeglass and examined the surface of the drawing. It was masterful. The deftness of touch, the ragged outlines, the *messiness*… This was not the work of a copyist but an artist. Pat Phelan had brought something to the table. Duval wondered what his own work was like. He touched a corner with his little finger and the pastel came off. Good, at least he hadn't used fixative. Sensible choice pastel, dry medium.

People had laughed at Donald Rumsfeld, but his famous distinction wasn't so stupid when applied to art. In matters of provenance you could have 'known knowns' and 'unknown unknowns', but an 'unknown known' was as questionable as a putative WMD and more open to inspection. Better, if you were going for a big name, to make a copy of a picture that was documented but lost. A 'once known known'.

He propped the pastel up against the wall. As a fake it was probably worth a grand; as a Degas it was worth upwards of £30 million.

"Art is a rum do," he mused out loud, "Turner was right."

Until two years before, Duval had been Head of Impressionist & Modern Art at London auction house RazzelleDeVere, but they had rewritten his job description during the credit crunch and given the post to someone younger and cheaper. His wife was working so they weren't on the street, but the independent dealership he had set up was taking time to establish.

With the new top-lit extension, if it wasn't leaking, he could at least show clients pictures at home. But London was awash with established dealers who were struggling as the auction houses swallowed more and more of their business. Not content with using guarantees to hook the sorts of nervous sellers who would previously have preferred private treaty sales, the big auction houses were moving into other areas of the market. In the past few years RDV, for example, had been operating as a dealership on its own account. The auction house had been buying in paintings by rising stars and sitting on them until opportunity knocked in the shape of a public gallery show that would raise the artists' profiles and their prices. Now it was taking a punt on ICE to become a major player in the contemporary art market.

The problem with historic art, for both dealers and auction houses, was that the supply of good stuff was drying up. And the private dealer's professional advantage – the leisure to chat up rich widows – would soon be nullified when the supply of rich widows with blue-chip art collections ran out. Now especially, in a harsh financial climate, collectors wanted gold-plated investments like the Giacometti *Walking Man* that recently sold at auction for £65m. That was the genuine article though, heaven knows, there were enough dodgy Giacomettis around. More than half the drawings in circulation were probably fakes. The artist's estate was fighting a losing battle.

None of this, though, bothered people like RazellDeVere's director Nigel Vouvray-Jones as long as they could go on shifting stock. Turnover was all that mattered now. Sack the experts and take on more marketing staff. Billionaire collectors in emerging markets – China, India, Russia, the Gulf States – didn't give a hoot about the educated views of experts, they preferred the soft sell approach of Miss Cassandra Pemberton with her Armani glasses and her Prada handbag.

Serve RDV right if he slipped one past them. They had it coming.

But fooling the auction house, he knew, would be the easy bit. Artists' estates presented a more serious problem. There was always the risk of running up against surviving relatives who could recognise an artist's handwriting in his brushwork. The auction houses pretended they could, but they were bluffing. Most of the current crop of 'experts' couldn't smell a rat up their own trouser leg, and they were now so desperate for throughput they hardly bothered sniffing.

Well, not altogether true – they looked at documentation. If an 'unknown known' suddenly appeared out of nowhere there would be questions asked and demands for paperwork. Where did it come from? What exhibitions had it been shown in? Why didn't it feature in any catalogues? Why no photographs?

Photographs were the sorts of hard proof you needed. But if a painting had been photographed it would be traceable to a collection. Unless, of course, the collection had subsequently been lost.

Duval jumped up and went over to his bookshelves. In the top left-hand corner, gathering dust, he found it: Volume II of the *Répertoire des biens spoliés en France durant la guerre 1939-45*, the record of Nazi war spoils assembled by the Bureau Central des Restitutions after World War II. Volume II dealt with paintings, tapestries and sculptures. He had brought it with him from Razzells when he left. They'd never miss it.

He flicked through the pages of muzzy black and white photos.

A Matisse *Odalisque*, £30m at today's prices. A Cézanne *Still Life with Compotier,* possibly as much as £40m. That would be greedy. He paused at a *Harbour at Collioure* by Derain. That was better.

The photo was faded but clear enough to make out the composition. The colours you could only guess at, though with Derain there was a fair amount of leeway.

It had been in the collection of the Meyer family in Paris. The perfect lost picture. The trouble was that as soon as it was 'found' the family would come out of the woodwork to claim it. Unless, that was, the family was lost too.

He had a bit of research to do.

Chapter IV

Daniel Colvin had only been at *Marquette* a month when the office politics started. Fay had asked him to report on a rumour that RazzellDeVere had been buying in paintings by Dirk Boegemann, represented until now by the Orlovsky Gallery, and were sitting on a pile of them waiting for his prices to rise.

The recession had come at a bad time for Boegemann, just when his paintings had passed the six-figure mark and were headed for the stratosphere. Now rumour had it that the State Gallery was planning a show. The State was normally wary of contemporary painting – its conceptual bona fides were always hard to establish – but Boegemann's ghostly monochromes wouldn't frighten the horses, and RDV were reputedly offering sponsorship.

Public gallery rubberstamps painter formerly represented by leading commercial gallery and currently being stockpiled by auction house. It all sounded distinctly dodgy to Daniel. He did a bit of scratching around, interviewed a few people – even got the elusive Jeremy Gaunt on the phone thanks to the director's PA mistaking him for a young architect working on the new State Gallery extension. Gaunt said nothing was planned, which amounted to a quote. Daniel's piece was filed and flat-planned when suddenly, without an explanation, Fay pulled it.

Daniel was sure Crispin Finch was behind it. Fair enough, he understood Finch protecting his turf. He'd been with the magazine since it started. But having one's first news feature spiked was not a good omen. And now Fay, who had been flirty before, was ignoring him.

At this rate he wouldn't be in the job past Easter, and he needed to keep it if he was going to finish his art history thesis. So he said nothing when he was shifted to a routine item about a British Council-funded touring exhibition called *East Goes West*, a collaboration between the State Gallery and Khaleej Museums Authority in the United Arab Emirates.

The exhibition paired young British artists with Middle Eastern contemporaries working in similar ways. Daniel ran his eye down the list of exhibitors. Mervyn Burke, he noticed, was twinned with a Lebanese artist called Salim Murr, who collected autographs of people called Muhammad. Jason Faith was matched with Iraqi artist Jahmir Zerjawi, who turned bombed-out buildings into installations. And Celeste Buhler was partnered by Iranian woman artist Afshan Zardooz, who had filmed herself in a white burqa against a white wall so that all you could see of her were her eyes.

From the illustration point of view, it wasn't promising.

Daniel opened one image after another. An empty bombed-out room, another room empty but for a disembodied pair of eyes, a sheet of paper empty apart from a signature.

There must be something better. He opened an image called *The Nile Feeds Itself*, and smiled.

It was a contact sheet of photographs by an Egyptian artist, Karim El Sayed, documenting the dismantling of a reed-and-daub hut. The first picture showed the hut with smoke curling through a hole in the roof; the last showed the ashes of the fire into which the final reeds have been fed. It was paired with Cordelia Markham's exploding shed.

Another one for the thesis on Sheddism. Daniel copied it onto a memory stick and slipped it in his pocket. It still surprised and delighted him to receive confirmation of the centrality of the shed to the history of art: an archetypal symbol of creation from Bethlehem on.

He filed the copy to Crispin and attached the image.

"Thanks," came a curt reply, "but why the shed?"

The piece was eventually published under the title 'Middle East Agreement Signed' and illustrated with two signatures – 'Muhammad' and 'Mervyn Burke'. The second signature was attached to *Coffee Ring No. 23*.

Chapter V

It was a Poussin day, with a lapis-blue sky and streaky puffs of white cloud sailing over The Shed of Revelation at the back of no. 15 The Mall.

How grand that sounded! It still amused Pat to say his address without adding the postcode. Since moving to the street all those years ago he'd discovered that it shared its name with a dozen Malls in London, not counting the one The Queen lived at the end of. There were Malls in Bexhill, Brentford, Bromley, Croydon, Dagenham and Surbiton, all of them laying claim to the definite article. Pat's was in Bounds Green, Haringey. He and Moira had moved to the area more than thirty years ago and brought Martin up there, if you could call it upbringing. Then Moira had pushed off, Martin had gone west and he had been left in sole occupation, an ageing bohemian beached in the 'burbs.

From his kitchen window Pat was distantly aware of an expanse of violet signalling to him from inside The Shed. With a sinking heart, he recognised it as the latest incarnation of the upper section of The Seventh Seal. Over the decades he'd spent tussling with that painting, it had been halfway round the colour spectrum and back. Now he saw with a sickening clarity that cobalt violet wouldn't do the job either.

He wished to God he'd turned it to the wall and tucked it in properly the night before. Now the wretched thing would be clamouring for attention on a Blue Orange morning when he needed to focus on the class. Pictures were like children, never left you in peace. Out of sight, out of mind was the only answer.

As he shaved around his goatee at the kitchen sink, the unforgiving light of the bright March morning revealed in the soap-spattered glass that his hair colour also needed attention. His barnet was starting to look like Davy Crockett's hat, with the black tips turning red then white as they neared his scalp.

Insufficiently realist, too expressionist. He picked up the bottle of Just For Men off the windowsill and shook it. Enough for the eyebrows, maybe, but they could wait. Who was he kidding? He was old enough to be Suzy's father. Ah well, he sighed contentedly, you never knew.

The Blue Orangers were the amateurs Pat taught in The Shed on Friday mornings. He'd started the class for the money, placing an ad on the community notice board in the local Budgens, but carried on for the love. The group had been coming in various forms for years, although it had only recently acquired its name.

It was Wolf, of course, who was responsible. Pat had set up a still life of apples and oranges in a bowl and was preaching his usual broken colour sermon, urging the class to under-paint in complementary colours that would break through the picture surface and make it quake. A fought-for image, Pat maintained, was an image worth having. But Wolf, a wartime refugee and a diehard pacifist, refused to fight on principle and persisted in painting his oranges orange.

Wolf insisted he could only paint what he saw; when he tried to make things up they just didn't work. (They didn't work that well when he didn't but Pat wasn't going to be the one to tell him.) Meddling with reality, he said, messed up the shadows and shapes needed shadows to hold them down. Without them everything sort of floated off. So while Pat had his back turned that particular morning, Wolf had tiptoed over to the table with a brush-load of ultramarine and painted all the oranges in the fruit bowl blue.

Pat was smiling at the memory when the phone rang.

At that hour of the morning it had to be Moira about money. She'd have it soon enough. He let it ring.

Late news from Marty was that his millionaire collector friend was cock-a-hoop about the Degas. Now, apparently, he wanted modern masters for his mansion and he'd given Marty a list of half a dozen. At three grand a pop Pat would be coining it. The downside was that the collector had now decided he wanted copies of existing works, which made Pat's job that much more boring to do. But he wasn't grumbling. If the guy could piss away that much on copies, what wouldn't he pay for the genuine article? The heptatych was in need of a home, or better a chapel. He wondered if there was room for a chapel in the mansion's grounds.

The lime green of Pat's trousers clashed briefly with the grass as he hurried across the garden carrying a safety lamp, a colander, a bunch of yellow fabric freesias and some purple tissue paper. The lamp had come from a neighbour's skip, the freesias from a church bazaar, the tissue paper from the offy and the colander from Dino's late mum. "The only thing she left me," the lugubrious Italian had lamented to him, "and it had holes in."

It had the makings of an interesting still life, Pat thought. The whiplash curve of the metal lamp hook certainly had dynamic potential. The flowers could have done with a vase, but there was always the coal scuttle. And the colander would have looked better with a load of apples, if he hadn't eaten them. Never mind, he'd fill it with coal from the scuttle.

Good colour combo, yellow, purple and black.

Inside The Shed The Seventh Seal assaulted his senses. In the light of day the violet was a complete disaster. For a moment last night he'd had the colours in perfect equilibrium, all the plates spinning in the air at once, then he'd trowelled on the violet and dropped the lot. Now the balance was shattered he'd have to scrape off.

He saw it now, too late, clear as mud. The whole thing

hinged on the mighty angel with a face like the sun and feet like pillars of fire. The angel had to burn up the competition, and by swamping everything in violet he had put the fire out. The hiss of the soggy embers brought him close to tears.

The morning after could be worse with paintings than with drink or women.

He turned the picture wearily to the wall and looked around to find Irene behind him. She had a feline knack of suddenly materialising.

"Hello old cat," he greeted her absently. "To what do I owe the pleasure?"

"You booked me for a session, remember?"

He didn't, but he hadn't the heart to send her away. She was probably counting on the money. So when the class arrived they found a model reclining on the yellow bedspread with a scuttle of flowers and an overhanging skip light.

Pat was dithering over where to put the colander full of coal. In honour of the lapis-blue morning he'd based Irene's pose on the sleeping nude in Poussin's *Nymphs and Satyrs* in the National Gallery, but the still life elements were giving him grief – though he liked the way the curve of the skip light hook rhymed with Irene's right breast.

He'd arranged the flowers in the scuttle with the tissue for foliage. The vertical flue of the wood-burner stood in for the tree under which Poussin's abandoned nymph luxuriates, and the skip light hung just to the right of the trunk where the face of Poussin's leering satyr peeks out. After trying the colander in several places he settled on a position in the left foreground, making a diagonal with the skip light through the nymph's head.

"Nude descending a chimney," quipped Wolf as he got out his paints.

"Got it!" said Pat. Still life problem sorted. He told the class to give it the Cubist treatment.

As they got stuck into the subject a hush descended, punctuated by the occasional squeak of charcoal and rattle of pencils in a case or brushes in a jar. It was the sound of parallel play not heard since childhood, the happy hum of absorption in the perfectly useless.

Naturally the Cubist theme went to pot. As hard as Pat tried to challenge his class to do things differently, they always ended up doing them the same. Wolf always produced the same naive paintings with glaring local colours and heavy black shadows. Suzy always turned out the same bright and breezy pictures on the safe, Scottish Colourist side of Fauve, with all the women looking exactly like her. Here she was, at it again, putting her own head on Irene's body.

But what a head it was, thought Pat, sneaking a sideways look at the heart-shaped face with its insouciant, slightly sniffy nose framed by floppy golden hair and dangly earrings. You could see the temptation.

Grant, meanwhile, created boxy 1950s abstracts out of whatever you put in front of him. He could have been staring into Marilyn Monroe's wide-open beaver and he would have filed it all away neatly into modular storage. The ordered mind of a solicitor, Pat supposed. And Dino... well Dino was just Dino. It was impossible to put a name to the amorphous splodges even now appearing on his canvas. If Dino's first artistic language was Italian, then he was a *macchiaiolo* with a speech impediment. Yet the deliberation he brought to his task was awesome. Look at him now, dotting in the holes in the colander with the same fevered concentration he had just applied to Irene's right nipple.

As for Yolande, Pat suppressed a sigh. Yolande was a one-trick pony with the stubbornness of a mule. Her approach to every subject was to home in on an area of detail – half an orange and the end of a banana, or a shoulder and an armpit – and blow it up to fill the entire canvas. She brought things so close to the picture plane you could have smelled them, if it had helped you to work out what they were. This morning she was focusing on the junction between the pink of Irene's exposed throat and chin and the galvanised steel grey of the background scuttle, with its protruding triangle of purple tissue. Wolf once joked that if you taped all Yolande's life drawings together they'd add up to one enormous, bill-board-sized nude. Yolande wasn't amused. The others had learned to put up with Wolf's jokes but Yolande didn't have a sense of humour.

The only member of the class who found Wolf funny was also the only born artist among them. Maisie was a natural. Pat had spotted her eye for colour in the charity shop, where she'd pick out clothes from the bags for him and hide them out the back. Maisie was in her 70s, she had never painted but she took to broken colour like a duck to water. Her drawing was erratic but her paint surfaces shimmered like Bonnard's. She *responded* to the subject. And sure enough, when Pat did the rounds, hers was the picture that thrummed with life.

He held it up for the group's admiration.

"All singing all dancing," he cried, "that's how we like our scuttles!"

Maisie peeped over the top of her glasses and smiled, a brittle little smile that lit up her face like an involuntary reflex. Suzy and Yolande looked deflated.

Pat went over to examine Suzy's painting. The skip light, scuttle and flowers were perfectly drawn and the treatment was Cubist, but the nude was young and slim with a turned-up nose.

As he looked from Suzy's nymph to Irene and back, he felt a dangly earring brush his cheek. He swallowed.

"It helps to look at the model from time to time," he said.

Chapter VI

The bright spring sun threw the giant shadow of a pterodactyl across the wall of the director's office on the top floor of the State Gallery.

The first time it had happened Jeremy Gaunt had jumped, but the crane had been working outside his window for weeks now and he was used to it. Eventually, he hoped, it would stop bothering him. With the foundations of the new extension only just laid, the pterodactyls would be nest-building for months. His main concern now was that the shadows kept moving. If they froze it meant the money had run out.

Adaptable creatures, human beings, got used to anything. How could Gaunt have guessed when he got his first regional gallery directorship in his thirties, a rising star in a newly legit-imised contemporary art world, that he would spend his fifties at the top of the gallery tree directing architects rather than artists? Then it was all about shaking up the British figurative art scene with cutting edge Minimalism imported from America. Now it was about shaking down American billion-aires to raise the funding for cutting-edge extensions.

He went over to the window and looked down into the foundations that gaped beneath him like a clutch of pterodactyl chicks waiting open-beaked for their mother to appear with food. And here she was returning to the nest with a 12m steel I-beam – another £3,000 worth – dangling from her jaws. At this rate the tens of millions of funding he'd wheedled out of a reluctant Department of Arts & Community Cohesion would be spent before the building showed above the ground. And in these lean times there'd be no more where that came from. The rest would all have to be got from private sources.

Meanwhile, of course, building costs were soaring. Spritzer & Camorra's egg-shaped design had seemed a nice idea during the boom years when galleries were sprouting extensions like designer fungi, but now it looked extravagant and unnecessary – which, in private, he was forced to admit it was. God only knew what they would fill the place with. The ostensible argument for government funding had been that the gallery needed more wall-space for its collections, but apart from the fact that the egg had no vertical surfaces, the State collection still consisted mainly of Victorian paintings that could never be hung in a modern gallery. So the space would have to be filled with a rolling programme of temporary exhibitions, which meant more curators and more marketing staff. More money.

As another I-beam sailed past the window, Gaunt thought back to the events of the night before. That business with Dirk and the redhead after the party had been a mistake. He could get away with that sort of thing in Basel but not here. If the story got out Virginia would never forgive him. Not that it would damage his reputation with the public; he was aware that people thought him sexless. Well, there was life in the old dog yet.

He felt his face muscles contract momentarily as he remembered the scene in Dirk's hotel room. He really ought to exercise them more often, then it might not look as if he had jaw ache every time he smiled. He was conscious of how unnatural it appeared. He'd caught himself in the mirror once and it had wiped the smile off his face.

Dirk was a liability, but he loved the guy. He was an artist, damn it, and he lived like one. He was generous too; he'd given the State a break on a group of barbed wire paintings. That didn't happen often. They owed him a show.

23

Gaunt had been around for long enough to remember the days when public gallery curators relied on their connoisseurship to acquire work cheaply at the start of artists' careers. You'd go to a studio somewhere in the sticks and buy a canvas fresh off the easel, still smelling of turps. Some artists you invested in never made it and were forgotten, others hit the big time and made up your losses. In those days acquisition budgets weren't a problem. Today the State's budget didn't go anywhere because it was competing in a global market for contemporary artists with established reputations. A national gallery had to stock the big global brands to keep its place in the international rankings. And that meant buying at the top of the market, competing with Russian oligarchs and Arab princes.

How could the State plug the gaps in its contemporary collection when as fast as one was filled, another one opened? Gaunt stared down into the foundations yawning beneath him as into the abyss. Artists were prepared to be generous, but only for as long as their profiles needed raising by representation in a national collection. If a national gallery lost its global cachet, the game was up. True, the State's new extension – when and if it opened – would create a buzz, but for how long? Another newer building would open elsewhere and Spritzer & Camorra's egg would be yesterday's omelette.

The single ray of light on the horizon was the emerging art scene in the Middle East. Acquisitions of Middle Eastern art would attract Community Cohesion funding, and prices hadn't yet caught up. They soon would. Prices for Indian art had surged; the State had missed that boat. But contemporary art from Islamic countries was still affordable. Without a traditional culture of art collecting, they were starting from scratch.

Gaunt picked up the *East Goes West* catalogue and was leafing through it when his PA buzzed him.

"Aldo Camorra on the line," she said. "Something about an eggshell finish?"

Chapter VII

A sea of bottle green broken with yellow, an expanse of pale red beach dappled with orange, a clutter of fishing boats hauled up above the shoreline, deep blue in shadow, orange in the evening sun. One boat coming in, another leaving for a night fish and various figures loafing on the shore watching the green of night descend to quench the yellow sun dipping behind the orange hills across the bay.

It didn't need the signature underlined by the distinctive tail on the 'n' to tell you that the painting was by Derain. It was one of a dozen seminal views of the harbour at Collioure painted during that decisive summer of 1905 that Derain spent with Matisse inventing Fauvism in the East Pyrenean fishing village near the Spanish border. It was what auction houses called a 'pivotal work'. They rarely appeared on the market and the last one to come up at Westerby's New York had sold for $12m.

This one, what's more, had a back-story to die for. It had been part of a Jewish collection of modern paintings seized by the Nazis in Paris in 1942 and added to the pile of art loot then being amassed at the Special Staff for Pictorial Art's HQ in the Jeu de Paume.

The Meyers' was not a big collection, but it was discerning. The Polish-born Joseph Meyer had adventurous taste. His fabric store in the Marais garment district didn't make him the sort of money needed to buy the big modern art names of the day. By the time he started collecting in the 1910s Cézanne, Van Gogh and Gauguin were out of his league and Matisse and Picasso were heading that way, although he did buy drawings. But artists one rung down the ladder he could afford. Like a genuine connoisseur, he understood that while artists of the first rank can produce duds, artists of the second rank can produce masterpieces. He bought top-notch works by what were then still affordable painters: Derain, Marquet, Modigliani, Vlaminck. His pictures were his children – his marriage was childless – and when he and his wife Lily died in Auschwitz, their collection was orphaned.

A single surviving nephew, Michael Slominski, had escaped from Warsaw on the last Kindertransport to leave for England in 1939 and eventually settled in Hampstead, where he scraped a living as a picture gilder and dealer in oriental antiquities. Michael had childhood memories of seeing pictures of his uncle's art collection in a photograph album belonging to his mother, Joseph's younger sister, and after the war he returned to Warsaw and traced the album, with other family keepsakes, to the possession of a former maidservant. But as he died in the early 1990s before the advent of the internet and digital databases of looted art, he had no way of discovering what had happened to the paintings. Nevertheless he made a will leaving the collection, along with the photograph album, to the Hampstead neighbour, Iris Goodman, who had looked after him during his final illness.

Now, during construction works for the new trans-European rail link through Stuttgart, the cache of paintings had come to light in the basement of a house due for demolition. How the collection had got there was a mystery. Modern paintings such as Meyer collected would have been designated by the Nazis as 'degenerate art' and, along with other 'ownerless' Jewish avant-garde art collections seized in Paris, would have been relegated to the so-called Martyrs' Room at the Jeu de Paume, earmarked to be sold for foreign currency to fund Hitler's Führemuseum of 'approved' European art in Linz. Banned as degenerate from entering Germany, modern collections 'abandoned' by Jews like the Meyers were dispersed in Paris and – unlike other Nazi loot later recovered from wartime storage in Germany by agents of the Allies' Monuments, Fine Arts and Archives programme – disappeared into international collections, from which many works were only now resurfacing.

But for some reason, according to inventories kept at the Jeu de Paume, the Meyer paintings were included in one of the last rail freight shipments out of Paris in 1944, headed for the Heilbronn salt mines north of Stuttgart. One possible explanation is that the German dealer charged with converting the pictures into foreign currency preferred, with the end of the war in sight and hard times ahead, to squirrel them away for himself. Among the dealers approved by the Einsatzstab Reichsleiter Rosenberg, the special task force appointed by Alfred Rosenberg to sort through the loot at the Jeu de Paume, there must have been some who nourished secret tastes in degenerate art. Not all of them can have shared the Führer's Sunday painter propensities – Expressionism, after all, was invented in Germany. But whatever the story, at some point before or after its arrival in Heilbronn the Meyer Collection became separated from the rest of the shipment. When the paintings were found in the Stuttgart basement they were still in an unopened crate bearing the original ERR label and stamp.

History might never know what had happened. Twenty years after Michael Slominski's death, Iris Goodman was confined to a care home in Battersea suffering from Alzheimer's. When first named as the beneficiary of Slominski's will she had initiated a search for the paintings, to no avail. Now her inheritance was to be sold and her only benefit would be an upgrade in accommodation to a 'studio care suite'. Her Australian brother-in-law, a solicitor in Sydney, had taken charge of matters. He had put the pictures into the hands of the

London dealer James Duval, one of the reclusive Slominski's few friends. Duval collected netsuke and Michael had found him a few bargains. He had also restored the gilding on some antique frames.

Some of the paintings had suffered damage in the damp basement and needed conservation. It would be a while before they reached the market. But the Derain looked as fresh as the day it was painted.

Chapter VIII

Up against the moody violet of The Seventh Seal, which Pat had yet to steel himself to scrape off, the Derain harbour painting looked startlingly bright.

He wondered if he might not have overdone it. He'd had a completely free hand with the palette, as the photocopy Marty had given him was black and white. But he'd spent several studious mornings with the Derains in the State Gallery and, allowing for the fact that the State's only landscape from the artist's Fauve period was a London painting of the Thames and therefore muddier, he reckoned he'd pitched the colours more or less right. By a happy accident he'd since come across a reproduction of a Collioure painting in an old calendar saved from a car boot sale, and had inched up the colour key to match.

The paint-handling he was pleased with; it had life. If it was broken colour you were after, Patrick Phelan was your man. Just as well, as Marty's photocopy was so small and blurry he'd had to improvise the brushwork. All the same, it was dull work copying. He'd had more fun with the Degas, but he wasn't grumbling. Three grand a pop was an absolute fortune, the sort of money he hadn't seen in years. Alright, if he was honest, ever. And Moira had come over all sweetness and light since he'd handed over the first wodge. She'd gone back to calling him by her pet name Feeley – he hadn't been called that in twenty years. Best of all he'd been able to go mad in Cornelissen's and splurge on handmade Michael Harding paints.

For a hit of colour you couldn't beat those babies; they packed a punch like Rocky Marciano. Too good to waste on a load of Collioure cobblers – Rowney's cheapo Georgian student range had been good enough for that. No, the Hardings were reserved for The Seven Seals. The tubes were lined up in their racing colours, ready for the off.

Normally when a painting was finished Pat turned it to the wall to stop it nagging. Even when grown-up and ready to leave home, pictures went on clamouring for attention. Inadequately launched young adults, was that what they called them? Just like Marty, still a child at 35. But the Derain was no child of his, so he wasn't bothered. When The Seven Seals were unveiled in all their glory, the little French Fauve would pale into insignificance.

Marty had mumbled something about a Modigliani, but until a photo materialised Pat was free. With the decks luxuriously cleared for the heptatych, the day stretched out before him like a willing woman.

Still, the usual tremor of anxiety heightened Pat's excitement as he turned the seven canvases round one by one and stood them around him in a half-circle like a choir round a choirmaster. A ragtag choir, raw-throated and under-rehearsed. He had to get them singing in tune and in unison. Would they?

The White Horse, The Red Horse, The Black Horse, The Pale Horse, The Souls of the Slain, The Great Earthquake, The Seven Angels: the seven seven-footers lining the walls of The Shed jostled for attention while he stood in the doorway and watched them.

"Well now, my troublesome beauties, which is it to be?"

Not The Seven Angels, he would let them lie; he was still smarting from his bruising of the week before. The angels and their trumpets were too much. The sea of glass mingled with fire worked, and Jerusalem like a rare jewel built of jasper, but those other gemstones with tarts' names – emerald, chrysolite, beryl – were over the top. The Seventh needed purification by fire. He'd come back to it another day.

Not The Pale Horse, either. He felt too sanguine for that this morning, ditto The Souls of the Slain. It was between the white, the red and the black horse and the earthquake.

He was in the mood for a shake-up. He went for the earthquake.

Sun black as sackcloth, full moon like blood and stars falling to earth as the fig tree sheds its winter fruit when shaken by a gale. Sky vanishing like a scroll rolled up, and four angels holding back the winds of the earth…

St John was the biz. In the midst of the maelstrom, it was the image of the fig tree that struck him. He had made it the focus of the picture, positioning it between the black of the sun and the red of the moon, with silver stars raining through its bare branches.

The sticking point was the sky vanishing like a scroll rolled up. He had considered slashing the top of the canvas and rolling it back a la Lucio Fontana, but slashing his way out felt like an admission of defeat. What went for Slasher Fontana wouldn't go for Feeley Phelan. Still, the fact remained that painting things appearing was one thing and painting them vanishing was another. How to paint absence? That was the Holy Grail, the colour that didn't exist. Rembrandt came close in his putty-coloured shadows, but Rembrandt's earth palette was too much of this earth for Pat.

He decided to start at the bottom where the great multitude stood with palm branches in their hands before the throne and the Lamb, and work up. Once the bottom was sorted, the top would sort itself.

As he squeezed out the rich oil colours from the new paint tubes onto his palette, Pat felt their intensity like a chemical shot in the arm. The only way was to go for it, no half measures.

"I know your works," he shouted aloud, "you are neither

cold nor hot. Would that you were cold or hot! So, because you are lukewarm, and neither cold nor hot, I will spew you from my mouth."

Quite right too, the bastards had it coming.

For the robes of the sealed made white in the blood of the Lamb he had chosen Naples yellow, hotter than white and, more importantly, louder. The multitude had to cry out in a loud voice, while the rich and the strong – the doomed – were skulking in their caves hardly daring to breathe for fear the Lamb heard them. The marvel of *Revelation* was that it touched all the senses: synaesthesia on a stick. Silence, though, was as difficult to paint as disappearance. If the sealed were yellow, what colour were the doomed?

Pat was vacillating between Payne's grey and indigo, testing them out in his mind to hear how they sounded, when the cadmium orange clang of cowbells broke in on his thoughts and threw out his calculations.

Hellfire and damnation! Ten o'clock on a Wednesday morning. Who could it be?

Not Ron. His neighbour's habitual line of attack was from the flank through the gap in the hedge. Ron never made formal complaints through official channels.

If he ignored the interruption it might go away. He squeezed out an inch of indigo, mixed in some ultramarine and tried it for size on the caves to the right. Their mouths fell away to infinity. Ha! He was just beginning to relish the ensuing silence when the orange clang cut in again from the veranda, louder this time.

Fire and brimstone!

He laid down his brush, wiped his hands on his fuchsia shirt and crossed the garden to the back door in the side alley. Through the fox-flap of broken planking at the bottom he could see a pair of policemen's boots.

Too late to beat a retreat, the policeman would have seen his.

He drew back the bolt, scraped the door open and found

himself looking at a young woman dressed in black with a camera bag slung over her shoulder. She had long dark hair and heavy square horn-rimmed glasses, and when she smiled she showed good strong teeth.

"Tammy Tinker-Stone," she held out her hand.

Pat stared at her blankly. Was she a model? Remove the glasses and all that black and she wasn't bad-looking. But he was busy now, she could come back later.

"I've brought the camcorder," she smiled, tapping her bag.

Now he remembered. Bugger. She was one of Marty's fashionable young artist friends, the woman who wanted to film him painting.

Why? And why in the name of Jesus had he agreed?

He led the way back to The Shed with a heavy tread. No one had ever seen all the Seals together and this bird with the bovver boots was a total stranger. But he'd promised Marty, and he owed him. No time to cover their modesty now.

The young woman stopped in the doorway.

"Wow," she said, "what is it?"

"It's a heptatych," mumbled Pat, "of The Seven Seals."

"Its amazing," she said, unpacking her camera and going straight for the jugular: The Seventh.

"I can see the water," she pointed at the sea of glass, "but where are the seals?"

Pat decided it was useless explaining.

"I haven't put them in yet," he said.

Chapter IX

In his office overlooking Leg of Mutton Yard, Nigel Vouvray-Jones scrolled down the list of consignments for June's Impressionist & Modern sale and pushed another Nicorette through the foil. The two patches he was already wearing weren't working. He needed a top-up.

February's Contemporary auction had gone better than expected, thanks to Warhol. OK, Warhol wasn't exactly contemporary – he'd been dead for a quarter of a century – but he was alive in spirit, and his Factory had been so productive during his lifetime that, despite his Foundation's best efforts to choke off supply, there was little danger of stocks running out.

If RazzellDeVere's Contemporary Art Department had depended on the living they'd have had to shut up shop. True, contemporary artists like Seth Poons and Cosmas Byrne who had gone platinum during the boom years were in no danger for now. The recession might have dampened the western appetite for art about consumerism, but in the east it was just taking off. The problem was that the new breed of international collector only wanted blue chip investments, and two blue chip artists didn't make a contemporary art market.

Even alpha dealers like Orlovsky were feeling the pinch. Bernie had enough stock in storage to singlehandedly keep the contemporary art market afloat for a decade, but unless he got top whack he wouldn't sell. Once prices in an artist had been allowed to fall, the market in that artist was finished. And what collector today would pay top whack for a conceptual piece by an artist like Jason Faith, even with an Ars Nova certificate attached? When it came to the crunch, concepts were two a penny. Today's art investors wanted a bigger bang for their buck – a goat with golden goolies, not an empty room. In the current economic climate, the only thing conceptual art had going for it was low storage costs.

For the moment oligarchs and sheiks were keeping the wheels oiled, but their potential as collectors was limited. You couldn't play to their intellectual snobbery. They were not art-educated or even art-educable, just simple souls who wanted something flashy on the wall. A Warhol celebrity screenprint or a Byrne petal painting on a gold ground, yes; a washed-out Boegemann canvas of barbed wire at Birkenau, no. In the present climate those big Boegemanns would only sell to museums, and to sell to museums they had to be seen in museums first. It was a Catch-22 situation. A lot was riding on the State Gallery show.

Gone were the days when city traders bought contemporary art as an investment and put it straight into storage with the bubble-wrap still on. Those guys were risk-takers who liked risky art – clever stuff that made something out of nothing, like them. Now what collectors wanted was security, the sort of security offered by timeless art that took more and more time for auction houses to source, since most of it was already in museum collections. And time between now and June was running out.

Vouvray-Jones ran a listless eye down the catalogue entries for the June auction, absently masticating the stiffening gum.

A Picasso pencil sketch of Dora Maar.

A late de Chirico *Piazza d'Italia* (1952), a poor imitation of early work.

Three Sisley landscapes, one of Argenteuil, pleasant enough but hardly showstoppers.

A Renoir still life of fruit in a bowl. Why paint apples when you could paint breasts? In the case of Renoir no nudes was not good news.

A Kandinsky abstract from the Bauhaus years – good – measuring 10x12cm – not so good.

A landscape by Soutine, not known for his landscapes and not known at all to many of today's collectors.

A Matisse charcoal sketch of a woman in a peasant blouse, a colourless drawing by the master of colour.

A late Picasso painting of those clapped out musketeers; if it wasn't priapic it wasn't Picasso.

A late Munch painting of a man in a cabbage patch; if it wasn't masochistic it wasn't Munch.

A murky paint-clotted Ernst from his wartime 'grattage' period.

A Giacometti painting of a *Tête d'homme* – anonymous face, seen one, seen 'em all – but at least the provenance looked sound. Something to be grateful for with Giacometti. A minor museum might buy it, but it wasn't exactly going to spark a bidding war.

A shaky Degas pastel sketch of a ballerina from the 1910s, when the wretched artist was three-quarters blind. What wouldn't he give for a mid-1880s nude?

A Modigliani portrait of a woman with her clothes on: get 'em off, darling.

A Rouault Pierrot – at least that and the Miró *Femme et oiseau* squiggle (late again) had a bit of colour. The Miró had three: red, yellow and blue.

Unfortunately any fool could see that most of the colour in the catalogue was in the illustrations of related works by the same artists. They might as well have saved money on printing and published it in black and white. "Ou sont les Fauves d'antan?" Vouvray-Jones despaired as he turned listlessly to Cassandra Pemberton's catalogue notes.

"Dora Maar, Picasso's legendary muse… sketched in a private moment in pencil on a scrap of paper. There is an immediacy to the choice of medium".

Bollocks. The woman didn't have a clue. Instead of drawing attention to the lot's inadequacies she was meant to disguise them. That was what she was paid to do. Buyers didn't need telling it was only pencil on paper, they could see that unfortunately. If it was black and white, her job was to supply colour. Diversionary tactics, my dear! Use your imagination! Yes, we can see the almond eyes and the long fingernails, but what's the subtext? The bimbo couldn't sell soap to a laundry.

He picked up the phone and barked: "Get Cassandra in here."

There was a pause while his PA tried to locate her.

"I don't give a monkey's fart in a colander if it's her lunch break, find her."

He spat out the nicotine gum into one of the lilies in the vase on the table, scrunched the flower around it and chucked it in the bin.

Cassandra Pemberton was RazzellDeVere's in-house editor. Her role was to spice up the sales catalogue notes submitted by the experts, edit RDV magazine and occasionally, when no one younger was available, pose for news stories beside a star exhibit. Since the recessionary rationalisation she also ordered the flowers, bought cigars for clients – though no longer for the director – and fixed Mrs Vouvray-Jones's hair and Botox appointments.

She appeared in the director's doorway with an expression on her purebred horsey features that said: "What is it now?"

It didn't suit her.

"When you applied for this job, you had some qualifications," Vouvray-Jones began. "Remind me what they were."

She stared.

"A degree in History of Art from Edinburgh University, and an-18 month internship at *Marquette*."

"Ah. And did you write anything during that time?"

She didn't reply, but her colour deepened and her jaw set.

"I understand that your multiple-choice generation has never had to master the English language. That's a minor disability these days; Mr and Mrs Oligarch's grasp of English isn't great either. But there is such a thing as sparkle, and this catalogue text," his mouse scrolled furiously up and down the page, "has all the fizz of a bucket of fomenting compost."

He closed the document with a snap.

"Sexed up and on my desktop tomorrow."

She stood in the doorway with her arms folded and looked at him. He noticed that, with indignation, her breasts went up a cup size.

"Try to remember, if you can, that we're 'in trade'. Auction houses are in the business of selling. The idea is to find buyers for this stuff," he waved a pair of Asprey's cufflinks at the computer.

She turned and marched out.

Nice arse, he acknowledged, would look good in the saddle. He was wondering if she wore a thong or camiknickers when the phone beeped.

"James Duval on the line," came the voice of his PA.

"Not now," he said. James always made him feel guilty.

"It's about a Derain painting – 'Coal-something Harbour'? – from a private collection, complicated story."

He got up from his chair. "Tell him I'll go straight over."

'I think the picture's in Germany.'

From James a photo would be enough.

"Put him through."

Chapter X

Karim El Sayed's Egyptian shack going up in smoke would make the perfect coda to Daniel's doctoral thesis, *Sheddism: A thousand years of the shed as symbol of transformation and renewal in Western Art*. At present the historical balance was too heavily tilted towards stables in Bethlehem. El Sayed's *The Nile Feeds Itself* would add weight to the contemporary side, along with Cordelia Markham's exploding shed and Peter Bunting's floating model.

Daniel was working from home this morning, having been told off to attend a Metropolitan Police briefing on museum security at the British Museum. Sounded riveting. Crispin Finch must really have it in for him. Since his Boegemann piece got spiked he'd had nothing but dead-end stories to work on, when he wasn't compiling exhibition listings or rewriting Bernice Stock's copy. Her report on Orlovsky's ICE party had been the usual fluff, trying to sound clever and only succeeding in sounding arch. When you took out the arch, the edifice collapsed.

Daniel was learning the hard way that reputations in journalism aren't made by writers, they're made by subs.

He backed up the document, shut down his computer and moved it away from the basement window – the *Evening Standard* had just nominated Finsbury Park as one of London's top ten burglary hotspots. Slipping his notepad into his pocket, he lifted his bike up the basement steps and set off for Bloomsbury.

The police briefing had been arranged by the Museums Association in response to a recent high-profile theft from a public gallery. In March thieves had broken into the East London Gallery and got away with a Lowry, a Stanley Spencer and a small Henry Moore bronze, among a number of works on loan from the British Council Collection to a temporary exhibition meant to introduce new audiences to art. It emerged later that the alarm had been playing up for months and rather than risk too many false calls – with the police now operating a 'three false calls and you're out' policy – the gallery had left the device switched off during consultation on a replacement. A month before the theft, a Lowry painting had hit the headlines when it sold at RazzelDeVere's for a record £3m. It was thought the thieves were opportunists rather than professionals. No trace of the missing works had been found.

As the loss was covered by the Government Indemnity Scheme, a message had come down from on high instructing the Met's Art & Antiques unit to put a bomb under the museum community. This briefing was the result.

Not surprisingly, the room was two-thirds empty and the few museum professionals who had turned up were sitting with smart-phones and tablets at the back hoping to carry on with business as usual. Daniel seemed to be the only member of the press who'd bothered to show. He went and sat in the middle at the front.

DC Yasmin Desai would be chairing a panel of security experts and insurance consultants, a Museums Association representative and someone from the Art Loss Register. Daniel was expecting an intimidating Asian matron in uniform when a slip of a girl in a navy trouser suit strode onto the platform. She had short unruly black curls, almond-shaped eyes behind black-rimmed glasses and something humorous about her mouth.

He got out his notebook with unexpected eagerness and sat with his pen poised, like a schoolboy in front of a favourite teacher. He listened attentively as she broke down the basics of museum security into three key elements: physical defences, electronic surveillance and people. It sounded surprisingly interesting. He took notes. When she handed over to the National Security Adviser of the Museums Council, his heart sank. The man droned on about accreditation standards, risk assessment models, manning levels, locking down procedures, emergency action plans and security audits. Then a private security consultant stood up and explained the principles behind 'perimeter and trap protection' and 'the secure box' theory, reviewed options for security screws and anti-bandit glass and expanded on the latest developments in object protection systems and audio-verification technology.

Daniel tried not to fidget with impatience. Any minute now the briefing would be over and she'd be gone. What could he do? He was supposed to be a journalist; ask for an interview. About what? Never mind what, he'd think of something. Whatever.

When she wound up the proceedings, he shot from his chair.

"Hi," he stopped her as she came off the platform. "Daniel Colvin from *Marquette* magazine. I'm doing a story on the lax state of museum security and I wondered if you had time for a chat?"

"If you make it quick," she said, "and you don't mind chatting over lunch. I'm hungry."

"Me too," he lied. He had no appetite.

They bought sandwiches from a café in Coptic Street and took them out to a table on the street. She sat down with hers facing the sun.

"Fire away."

He played for time by getting out his notepad, snapping off the elastic and searching for a pen. The only questions on his mind were about her. How old was she? She looked 25 but to be a constable he figured she had to be 30. And her eyes were green. Where did that come from?

OK, security. He began with figures. What were the statistics for thefts from British museums in the past year?

She rattled them off too fast for him to take them down.

"I'm a bit of a Carol Vorderman with figures," she laughed. "I should have been an accountant. That's what you get from operating a till in your parents' corner shop when you're still in nappies." When she looked up, the sun caught the hazel in her irises. He noticed with regret that her photochromic lenses were darkening. He focused on her mouth.

So where did paintings by famous artists go when they were stolen? Presumably they were too recognisable to sell?

"People like to fantasise about them ending up in underground vaults belonging to billionaire baddies, but the truth is usually a lot less glamorous. Billionaires don't need to steal art, they can afford to buy it, especially at the level of the East London pictures. Above that level the best examples are in museums, so there might be a motive for some unofficial deaccessioning, though if you wanted the world's greatest paintings for your secret gallery it would be easier to commission fakes. None of your billionaire baddie friends would know the difference – and neither, to be honest, would half the auction house 'experts'."

"So why are famous paintings stolen?"

He hadn't touched his salt beef sandwich. She had finished her prawn and mayo and was looking unnervingly straight at him.

"Often because they're there, like Everest. They're stolen to use as bargaining chips or for collateral, sometimes for status. To a criminal, art is just another form of currency. That's how they see it portrayed in the media, where most of the time the only things you're told about a picture are the name of the artist and how much it's worth. A picture doesn't have to depict a dollar sign, like Warhol's silkscreens, for its message to be money. There are a lot of people for whom Van Gogh's *Irises* mean $54m – and that includes collectors and auction houses."

He was surprised by how much she seemed to know about art. He hadn't expected that from the Art & Antiques unit.

"How about ransoms?"

"They're illegal in this country. Officially museums aren't allowed to pay them... though what insurers do in private is their own affair."

She was finishing her drink and he'd run out of questions. He gripped his pen, sensing that if he put it down she'd reach for her bag and the interview would be over.

"How did you get into this business, if you don't mind my asking?"

"What's a nice Asian girl like me doing in the police?"

He squirmed.

"It's a long story, but if you really want to know I'll give you the edited version. This is not for your article, by the way."

"Off the record," he smiled and put down his pen.

Yasmin Desai was born into a Ugandan Asian family, originally from the Punjab. In 1972, expelled from Uganda by Idi Amin, her parents had sought refuge in Leicester and opened a corner shop. She was bright at school, taking Maths 'O' Level two years early, and her parents dreamed of a glittering career in accountancy. But Yasmin was mad on art and, as a strong-willed only child, she got her way – and quickly regretted it. She had a horrible time at Birmingham School of Art, where she lasted a year.

"Why?"

"The tutors hated my work. I was painting my life in the style of Indian miniatures and they said I needed to find a style of my own. They said my work was unoriginal and not 'contemporary'. Most of my year were making videos and installations. And then, to cap it all, I got pregnant."

Her parents were surprisingly good about it. They might have forced her into a marriage with the father, but fortunately her family was Hindu and he was Muslim so they didn't. And of course they both fell in love with Sami when he was born. But she knew that living at home as a single mother brought shame on her parents, and she was desperate to move out.

"To be able do that, I needed a job. The police were having a recruitment drive in Leicester for ethnic minority officers, and I signed up. My parents looked after Sami while I did my training, and after completing the probationary period I heard of a vacancy for a special constable in the Met's Art & Antiques unit. I applied, and got it. The art training came in useful after all."

She rose through the ranks to Detective Constable and scraped together the mortgage on a small flat in Walthamstow, where she was now living with Sami, aged nine.

"Do you still paint?"

'When I've got time." Her mouth turned down at the corners. "I've got a website," she added almost as an afterthought, pulling out a brightly illuminated card and handing it to him.

"What about you?"

"I don't have a website or a card. I'm an art historian. I'm working part-time for *Marquette* while I finish my thesis."

Before she could ask what the thesis was about and laugh, as people invariably did, he posed another question.

"What's your professional opinion of an art market in which auction houses and commercial galleries raise the prices of contemporary artists by procuring them prestigious exhibitions in public galleries?"

"That's a big question."

She thought about it.

"Personally I think it sucks, but it's legal. The same applies to a lot of practices in the art market. Regulation is so light-touch it's non-existent. But our job in the police is to enforce the law."

* * * * * *

The first thing Daniel did when he got to the office was to fish out Yasmin's card and check her website. Up came an Indian miniature of a Nativity scene with the Virgin Mary and two midwives, but no Joseph. The Virgin had Yasmin's face and the stable was a garden shed at the bottom of a crazy-paved suburban patio.

Bull's eye! He had the perfect reason to see her again. Her picture would make an exotic addition to the Stable section of the Sheddism thesis. He'd wait a decent interval, then email her to ask to see the original.

What was a decent interval? The day after tomorrow. He'd have to confess about the Sheddism, but he had a funny feeling she might not laugh.

Chapter XI

Another Blue Orange morning, and The Shed was humming with creative concentration as the class got stuck into a new subject. No life model today, just a yellow vase of blue fabric hydrangeas Maisie had brought in from the charity shop. She had made her entrance, to applause, like a pension-age Flora with blooms bursting from the top of her tartan shopping trolley. Pat had wanted to paint *le tout ensemble* just as it was – a senior citizen's mobile cornucopia – but the Stewart tartan fought with the blue flowers, and when Maisie pulled out the yellow vase – to more applause – the colours sang.

Unused to being the centre of attention, Maisie was relieved when the fuss died down and she could unpack her painting gear in peace.

With the subject sketched in, the class were soon busy with the underpainting. Suzy had chosen magenta for her flowers and viridian for her vase; Yolande went for cadmium red and Davy's grey. Wolf's flowers were blue and his vase was yellow. Dino hadn't reached the colour stage; he was stuck on the drawing trying to get the flowers to fit in the frame. At the moment his vase took up two-thirds of the canvas and his flowers were cut off halfway up the stems. He rubbed the drawing off with a rag and started from the top. Grant had covered his whole canvas in raw sienna and was squinting at the subject, abstracting its essence.

Maisie mixed a delicate shade of orange and started dabbing in flower shapes in soft clouds of colour, looking over her glasses to judge the effect as if broaching a sensitive topic and anxious not to overstep the mark.

Pat wasn't his usual self. He was distracted, and it wasn't by Suzy's skimpy crop top. After the interruption by the video woman – for whom he'd put on a star performance, though he said so himself – he'd gone full throttle on The Seven Seals, and for a day and a night he'd been on fire. The angels holding back the winds of the earth had achieved sublimity and the great multitude had finally given voice, in yellow. With the Sixth Seal all but sewn up he'd switched back to the Second and put a bomb under the red horse of war. This time the old nag that previously refused at every fence had sailed clean over with the wind behind it, taking peace from the earth and leaving blue murder in its wake. But now, just when he had got up steam to nail the Seventh, Marty had started pressuring him for more copies. He'd threatened to come round today with another couple of photocopies – a Modigliani nude and a Marquet landscape – and he was talking about a Jawlensky and a Vlaminck too. How many pictures did one collector need? With that much wall space he could accommodate the Seals.

Pat could take or leave the money; he didn't have a habit to support. Money meant he could get a plumber to fix the leaky sink, but a bucket had done the job perfectly well for years. It meant he could stand Dino drinks in the pub and splurge on books and records in Maisie's shop. Last time he was in there he'd found a pair of sealskin boots which if they'd fitted he would have bought. But the only real advantage of money, apart from keeping Moira happy, was that it put him in the fast lane for art materials. In the pigment stakes he was up there with Auerbach. Wasting good paint on copies, though, was like feeding caviar to the cat.

Speaking of cat food, this whole business was beginning to smell fishy. Things often did when Martin was involved. If it was copies his collector wanted, why the black and white photos? Colour photos would have made more sense. And now Marty was hassling him over drying times. Why the hurry, when his collector friend could bung the daubs up on the wall fresh off the easel and tell the maid to hold off on the feather dusting?

Marty had always been that way, long before the drugs. When he was a kid Pat and Moira had found it funny, little Marty wheeling and dealing in the playground and coming home with a pack of water balloons or stickers. Now he was dealing coke and snorting half of it up his nose. Pat blamed himself, he should have given him more attention but between the night jobs and the painting he never had time. And Moira, sweet lovely Moira, was a pushover.

Talk of the devil, here was Marty now crossing the garden with that bouncy walk which in his father's long experience spelt trouble. Pat shot out of The Shed to intercept him. He didn't want him blabbing about the copies in front of the class; that would be embarrassing. But Martin insisted on breezing in.

"Hi guys," he said, looking around and smiling at Suzy.

He handed Pat an envelope marked M&M with a meaningful look and took a turn around the room.

"Nice," he leant over Suzy's perfectly tanned shoulder, watching her pink hydrangeas turn blue at the edges and yellow highlights flash from her emerald vase. "Interesting," he stood behind Grant and directed a critical eye from the brown of the canvas to the blue of the flowers and back. He paused behind Dino and scratched an ear, paused behind Wolf and rubbed his nose, and stopped at Maisie. "Lovely," he said and sounded like he meant it. He avoided Yolande, who was looking daggers at him.

Pat hustled him out, but not before he'd stopped at the stack of large canvases leaning against the wall by the entrance and turned the topmost one around, to a burst of violet.

The class all interrupted their painting to look.

"The Seventh Seal," Pat mumbled uncomfortably, "from Revelation".

He wanted to forestall any questions about marine mammals, but only succeeded in prompting a joke from Wolf: "In my day, Revelation was a make of suitcase."

Yolande glared at Wolf, but no one else bothered to respond.

"You've got an asset in that class," Martin shouted up at the veranda as he bounced back across the garden. "If you put them all to work we could step up production."

Chapter XII

It wasn't necessarily his fault. So digging out the gym under Mervyn Burke's Hampstead house had affected the water table, but the house next door might have subsided anyway. It was on a hill.

Martin put the letter face down on the kitchen counter and flicked on the kettle for a coffee. He noticed the signature on the back read 'Mervyn Burke' rather than the usual 'Merv'.

His friend was not in a friendly frame of mind. The letter was to tell him that his next-door neighbour, an eminent QC, was taking him to court.

Martin was a glass half-full kind of guy, but recently his optimism level had been sinking. For a blagger he couldn't complain, he'd had a good run. The jump from builders' labourer to interior architect had taken brass balls, with which he happened to be generously endowed. What he didn't happen to be endowed with, right at this minute, was brass. He couldn't pay his landlord, let alone his dealer. It embarrassed him to have to subsidise his habit by scoring for Godfrey's toy boy; it was beneath him.

The work had dried up, unlike the damp in Orlo's orangery. Interior architect by appointment to the contemporary art world had been a cushy gig while it lasted, but he'd run through his entire circle of acquaintance and they weren't coming back for more. Nor, he suspected, would they be providing references. And new clients would expect qualifications.

If the old man would only pull his finger out they could get the ball rolling, but yesterday's visit had confirmed Martin's suspicions that instead of getting on with the paying commissions his dad was secretly back at work on those Seven Seals. Tammy had filmed him at it only last week.

How long had he been fussing over those paintings? Half a lifetime. Martin had memories of coming home from school and finding his dad holed up with them in the bedroom while his mum was at work. He still felt a residual sting of resentment at the memory of having had to get his own tea. And here the old man was now, with orders waiting to be filled and money to be made, shut up in his studio footling away at their tender bits.

The trouble with his father was he never needed money. He had always managed to survive somehow on air.

Any normal person would have seen the pointlessness of finishing pictures that would never find a buyer. Who was going to give houseroom to seven seven-foot canvases by an artist who'd reached retirement age without ever making it? Serious dealers didn't take on artists over 40, they needed the early years to build the brand. Anyway his dad was the wrong sort of artist. There was too much feeling in his work. It was embarrassing. Wealthy collectors didn't want emotional overload dribbling down their walls, they wanted art they could safely ignore. Fine for Francis Bacon to let it all hang out, he was famous and dead, but who was going to tolerate an unknown living artist exposing himself all over their house? Plus if the pictures weren't worth tens of millions of dollars, how would rich collectors explain the investment to their friends? They'd have to say they bought them because they liked them. God forbid.

For the first time in his life Martin felt depressed. He was almost in danger of losing faith in himself. If it had been left to him the whole damn lot would have been done and dusted in pastel, but James insisted that only Degas used it regularly. With most other artists the medium was an exception, and exceptions were what they wanted to avoid.

James had the patience for the long game, but Martin was already tired of watching paint dry. What he'd had in mind was a Warhol factory knocking them out. He'd have done the job himself, but he wasn't an artist.

As he cut the last line of coke on the glass chopping board, the smell of onions from last night's fry-up overpowered him; his eyes were streaming as he poured the coffee and set the mug down on the kitchen counter.

When his vision cleared he found himself looking at a coffee ring stain with the signature 'Mervyn Burke' above it.

Think of a number, any number... Martin found a pencil and wrote 'No. 23' in the bottom right hand corner.

Chapter XIII

Everyone who was anyone in Pickton-on-Tees was at the launch of the new Pickton Art Foundation, or *pAf* as it had been expensively branded by fashionable graphic design consultancy Value+Added.

For a century since the owner of the local steel mill, Ivor Dyce, had left his collection of English paintings to the city, the city fathers had been planning to build a museum. But after the steelworks closed and Pickton achieved the statistical distinction of being ranked the most economically vulnerable city in Britain, the city fathers had more important things to think about. And nobody else in the country was going to think about it, if Pickton ever impinged on their thoughts at all.

Pickton-on-Tees had fallen off the map, as had many of the British painters in the Dyce Collection. Pictures of sheep, potato pickers, shadowy barn interiors and dusky farmyards were kicked into the long grass during the Great War by Roger Fry and his fellow-disciples of Post-Impressionism. Who now remembered Sir George Clausen, Sir John Arnesby Brown and Joseph Farquharson – or Frozen Mutton Farquharson, as he was called, after his trademark paintings of sheep in snow?

And these were the Royal Academicians. Dyce had been a genuine patron. He also bought from young painters he had never heard of, most of whom have not been heard of since.

While the collection was 'temporarily' housed in an Edwardian villa on the outskirts of town, determined art-lovers would make the occasional visit, and the profound silence of the musty rooms with their mullioned windows would be momentarily disturbed by the creaking of a floorboard or the buzzing of a rudely awakened fly. Since the art lovers of Pickton could be counted on the fingers of two hands, the silence was not disturbed very often. But one habitual disturber of the peace was Gilbert Wise, a local doctor and keen amateur painter who used to take his little boy Godfrey with him.

On Godfrey's young mind that echoey house with its rooms filled only with paintings, and the occasional straight-backed chair, made an indelible impression. A particular favourite was the Farquharson of a wintry sunset with sheep and trees casting long shadows on the snow.

When he grew up, he resolved that he would have his own art collection – and he did, though it turned out differently from Dyce's. In the Godfrey Wise collection the place of Joseph Farquharson's sheep immortalised in paint would be taken by Cosmas Byrne's preserved in formaldehyde.

By the time Godfrey had made the second billion from his discount stores, Wise Buys, art collecting had entered a period of seismic change and he was swept along on the tsunami. He wasn't a dabbler like his father and, if he was honest, he couldn't tell a good painting from a bad one. On the few occasions when dealers took him to meet painters in their studios they spoke a language he didn't understand and he got the feeling, even when they were northerners, that they looked down on him.

Paint was a slippery substance Godfrey couldn't get hold of. When a painting was about something, he was on the ball – you knew where you were with Frozen Mutton Farquharson – but when a painting was about paint he was out of his depth. He was an entrepreneur, a man of ideas, and ideas were what he looked for in his art.

Even before Charles Saatchi's 1997 exhibition *Sensation* propelled a new generation of conceptual artists into the mainstream, Godfrey had started collecting contemporary art. Storage space was not a problem; he had warehouses and he filled them. He went to the newly opened East End galleries, he went to the parties, he felt accepted in a way he had never felt in Cork Street. And while his devoted wife Shirley minded her hairdressing business in Pickton and kept the home fires burning, he found himself spending more and more time in London indulging his newly discovered weaknesses for cocaine, GHB and interestingly damaged arty boys.

The Wise Buys warehouses, meanwhile, were filling up with art acquisitions, still bubble-wrapped and crated, that he couldn't show. Mrs W refused to have the stuff in the house, apart from a Cosmas Byrne petal painting on a gold ground that she allowed into the living room. Then one afternoon at Pickton Golf & Country Club's 19th hole Godfrey was approached by the head of local Regional Development Agency 'Capital Ts' with a proposal.

Money was available from the European Regional Development Fund, Renaissance in the Regions, VisitTeesside and the Northern Bank Foundation to build a landmark gallery that would put Pickton on the cultural map and turn it into an art tourist destination. But between Godfrey and the gatepost, the problem was the Dyce Collection. In a new steel and glass gallery it wouldn't *go*. Besides, to put it baldly, who was going to travel up from London to look at so many paintings of shadowy barns and sheep?

They'd have to show them, of course, as the collection belonged to the city and local people expected that sort of art. They could give over a room to rolling displays. But for the main galleries they needed cutting-edge art to demonstrate that Pickton was a happening place where companies with vision should be investing. Would Godfrey consider lending works from his collection? Once the gallery was up and running, money might be found from the Contemporary Art

Association and NAF – the National Art Fund – to help build a contemporary collection of small affordable pieces. But what they needed now, to get attention, was the big stuff.

It had been a marriage made in heaven, and Godfrey was now standing on a dais in the shiny new building it had engendered. On a sunless day in May the vast atrium with its north-facing wall of glass felt unseasonably chilly – heating had been low on the Italian architect's list of priorities – and Shirley Wise's shoulders stiffened slightly under her bouffant hair as she listened to her husband speaking with affection of the formative influence on him of the Dyce Collection. She liked paintings of the countryside and was pleased the collection would have a proper home, though apparently the paintings wouldn't be on show until later in the year in case they gave the wrong initial impression. The inaugural show was titled *A-R-T: The Future Is Here* and drawn entirely from her husband's collection.

There were speeches from the director, the mayor and the head of the Regional Development Agency, who predicted a bright future for the gallery as an art destination of national and international stature. A town of which it had once been said that the most exciting thing to do of a Sunday afternoon was watch the traffic lights change now had the major attraction of a modern art gallery. And where there was art, as sun follows rain, employment would follow.

* * * * * *

Daniel decided not to wait for the speeches to finish. If he slipped around the galleries discreetly now he'd be back at the station in time for the 7.38 to London. It shouldn't take long, just a case of ticking artists off a list. Normally *Marquette* would have sent Bernice but Pickton-on-Tees didn't register on her party radar, which was sensitive enough to pick up a signal from the Gwangju Biennale. Her radar was right. None of the artists showed.

Daniel made a cursory stock-check round the galleries. A Cosmas Byrne bisected sheep and a suite of screenprints of pills in sherbet colours titled after Stations of the Cross. (Wise also owned a Byrne petal painting, but his wife had apparently refused to relinquish it.) A lipstick-pink Stacey Nassim neon sign reading *Love Yourself* above a wall of scratchy masturbation drawings. A Mary Jonas ashtray made of fag ends. A Tammy Tinker-Stone film titled *Fire! Little Liar* that played backwards to show firemen sliding up a pole to the accompaniment of a choice of interactive soundtracks: on a red jukebox in the shape of a fireman's cab visitors could select between the *Fireman Sam* song, Derek and Clive's *The Fireman Song* and Lil Wayne's *Fireman*.

This one would be a hit with the kids. Tables in the Education Room upstairs were already spread with Fireman Sam colouring sheets for younger visitors, and the gallery shop was stocked with Fireman Sam pencils and Jupiter fire engine sharpeners.

On a subtler note, there were minimalist interventions in the gallery space. Jason Faith, for his *Opus Number 97*, had removed the overhead LED bulbs from the gallery lift, leaving the illuminated buttons B, G, M, 1 as the only sources of light. Faith was also responsible for *Opus Number 98*, a traffic light system on the toilet doors that flashed red for occupied, green for vacant and amber when the flush was activated. Above the lockers in the cloakroom hung Celeste Buhler's spatial intervention *White Elvis*, a white plastic clothesline holding a pair of girl's white cotton pants with the words 'THE KING' embroidered in white across the front. It was also Buhler who had stretched the dressmaker's measuring tape with all the numbers tippexed out along the edge of the counter in the ground floor café. Titled *The Measure of All Things*, it was part of her ongoing series *Everything's All White*.

By the time Daniel reached the Drawings Gallery on the mezzanine with its view of the town hall car park, the speeches were over and the guests were on their way upstairs, the clatter of high heels on the slab glass stairs mingling with stifled squeals of merriment from the lift.

The Drawings Gallery contained a single image, the first acquisition in *pAf*'s permanent collection of works on paper, bought with a grant from the Contemporary Art Association. The trustees had chosen to inaugurate the collection with one of Mervyn Burke's ephemeral series of *Signature Works*, executed in a range of impermanent media including the artist's semen, snot and blood – DNA markers that would fade with time, leaving the artist's signature as the only visible trace of their passing. The medium of this *Signature Work* was relatively safe and uncontroversial – the only bodily fluid it contained was possibly saliva mixed with the coffee that had left a ring stain on the slightly crinkled paper. It was signed and numbered 23.

Funny, thought Daniel, he could have sworn that was the number of the Burke *Signature Work* Crispin had chosen to illustrate his piece on *East Goes West*. He was unlikely to have misremembered. Twenty-three was his lucky number.

Before he could make his exit the lift doors opened and *pAf*'s newly appointed director, Marjorie Rimmington, emerged blinking into the light with a group of eminent Picktonians in tow.

She made straight for the Burke.

"This is the gallery's first acquisition," she announced proudly. "We were lucky to get it for a special price from a friend of the artist who received it as a gift. Mighty oaks from little acorns grow, and great collections from little coffee beans..." Her pause for laughter met with an awkward silence. "Pickton is playing its part in redefining drawing. Our ambition is no less than to become the go-to gallery for post-modern works on paper in the North-East."

As Daniel slipped out through the glad-ragged gathering of Pickton's finest, he wondered whether the city's 6,500 unemployed wouldn't rather spend their free afternoons observing changes in the traffic lights than redefining drawing. But he knew better than to write that in his article.

Chapter XIV

Duval should have seen it coming. First the new bathroom with the Brazilian blue marble vanity top. Then the new kitchen with the stainless steel cabinets. Then the conservatory with a cupola, which leaked.

The demands had been escalating, and now Valerie had asked for a divorce. She'd get the house, of course, and without that he was finished. Bad enough to be a dealer without a gallery, but a dealer of no fixed abode? Forget it.

In the last of the evening light, the tarp on the cupola cast a subaqueous gloom over the conservatory. Duval smiled bitterly. He had entered his Blue Period. How had it come to this without him noticing? Incrementally, as it always does, bit by bit.

Looking back over his life, it was blindingly obvious that at every juncture he had taken a wrong turn. If he'd opted for the academic career that quite clearly awaited him he'd be safely ensconced by now in some professorial pigeonhole, a respected authority, dusty but distinguished, on a regular salary with a university pension. Instead of which where was he, the precociously brilliant student who had passed out top of his year at the Courtauld for a thesis on *Expressionism and the Primitive* that went straight into publication (Cherwell & Cam 1980) and landed him a job as the youngest ever head of department at RDV?

Out of work, out of marital favour, out on his ear. What had happened to all that youthful promise? Evaporated, frittered away, wasted.

He got up and emptied the bucket under the cupola into the wilting begonia, before shifting the begonia under the leak and removing the bucket.

Whatever had made him think he could go into business, an innocent like him? He completely lacked the killer instinct needed for survival in the art world, a flatfish in an aquarium full of sharks. And now he had sunk to mixing with bottom-feeders like Martin. He had chosen a career to which he was psychologically totally unsuited: he had no interest in money and he loved art.

If he contested the divorce, he might be able to delay proceedings. If the case didn't come to court for a few months and he held out until the October sale at RDV, he could give Valerie the money to buy her own house. For the time being he was just about OK sleeping on the chesterfield in his study, letting himself in the back through the alley door. As long as he had the run of the basement, he wouldn't need to put his pictures into store.

The last Derain to sell at Westerby's New York had raised £12m. That would give Valerie enough to buy a small palace and clad it inside and out with marble and steel. The alimony he could sort out later. By then Phelan would have delivered the Modigliani and perhaps the Marquet, and it would be a matter of waiting for the odour to fade. Varnishing helped, but it would take six months.

Nigel had been pressuring him for the Derain in June, but he'd resisted. He half regretted returning that Degas pastel to Martin. It would have been a risk, but it was ready money.

Like Martin, he was losing patience with watching paint dry.

Chapter XV

The brittle click of plastic on plastic came from the editor-in-chief's office as the freshly applied nail extensions of Fay Lacey-Piggott – FLP to her troops – made contact with her computer keyboard. Like any dactylographer from the pre-electric era, Fay struck her keys with determination; it was the one clue to her age she could not correct. The eyelids, chin and teeth had all had attention. The figure, naturally scrawny, was still youthful, although the gym-toned upper arms were a tad too muscular.

In happier days Fay had spent her mornings on the phone and her afternoons lunching, but no longer. Since the editor and deputy editor had been let go she had had to step into the breach, writing, editing and even subbing copy.

This morning she was rewriting Bernice's piece on the launch of Orlovsky's new space in a Moscow multi-storey car park. So far, not a single name of a Russian oligarch had been spelt right and some were so wrong they were beyond recognition by Google. If it wasn't for Bernice's contacts, she'd be next for the chop.

To be honest, it would have been simpler and more cost-effective to write Bernice's stuff from scratch oneself, if one had time to go to all the parties. But the parties themselves were getting boring. Did anyone actually care any more what Jason Faith said to Mervyn Burke at what private view or what white ensemble Celeste Buhler wore to what gallery opening? The party was almost over for the Cool British Artists. It was time for Bernice to update her address book, but first she needed to learn how to spell.

Through Fay's glass door the open-plan office looked busy enough, with well-dressed young women flitting to and fro. One commodity in superabundant supply in a recession was interns, but a magazine cannot live by interns alone. Someone's got to turn out usable copy. Last week the Venezuelans had cancelled the inaugural Caracas Bienal, and this morning two of the participating galleries had pulled their advertising. Add in the interview with the Bienal's director that would have to be spiked and that was two pages that needed filling before the magazine went to press tomorrow.

Too late to cut pages from this issue, but if the advertising didn't pick up next month they'd drop four pages of editorial, possibly eight. Hopefully readers wouldn't notice, with the extra padding of the Middle East supplement – assuming the advertising came in for *that*. But it would. There was no recession in the Gulf and the Arabs were desperate to establish themselves as major art world movers and shakers – or should that be sheikers? Fay wondered if that was too cheesy to use in a heading... Supplements were an advertising lifeline. The ad manager was already asking where next.

Through her door Fay could see Daniel hard at work, eyes glued to his screen. In her present predicament she was glad of the young man's help; he was cheap and efficient and he turned in readable copy, as long as he could be kept out of trouble. She'd get him to expand that report he was writing on *pAf* to a full page. Do an interview with Godfrey Wise and get a few quotes from the gallery director, the architect, the restaurant chef even – wasn't it a branch of Bercy's or something, the only one north of the M25? Crispin would whinge but he couldn't have his by-line on every feature. Crispin was becoming an old stick. And the gallery might be persuaded to take an ad, at a special introductory discount if they were too impoverished to afford the rates.

Watching the look of concentration on his handsome young face, Fay felt almost maternal towards Daniel. As she crossed the office to talk to him about the *pAf* feature she noticed him quickly clicking a webpage shut, but not before she'd caught a glimpse of Indian miniatures.

"A bit traditional for us, no?"

"I was thinking," said Daniel, blushing, "that with the record prices achieved at Westerby's Indian art auction this month it might be interesting to do something on artists of Asian origin working in Britain. Who'll be the next Daneesh Shakoor?"

An Indian supplement dropped into Fay's mind like a paper on a mat. This young man was turning out to be quite an asset. He had the instincts of a successful journalist.

Chapter XVI

Martin sighed as he adjusted his boxers and studied the squirt of jism on the virgin sheet of Fabriano Artistico hot-pressed watercolour paper. He was dimly aware of his dad's Degas nude looking down reprovingly from the chest of drawers, as if piqued that he wasn't fantasising about her.

"You're a bit old for me, love," he said and turned her respectfully to the wall.

It looked a bit of a mess, if he was honest. You had to hand it to Merv, his semen drawings looked drawn whereas his own effort looked, well, for want of a better way of putting it, come. There was more art to this game than he'd given him credit for.

At the risk of wasting expensive paper he tore off the soiled sheet, laid it on the bedside table and, with the tip of a nail file, scraped off a dollop of semen and carefully applied it, with a circular wrist action, to a fresh piece of paper.

It didn't look like Merv's work – he was more of a brush than a palette knife man – but it looked all right if he held the pad up sideways to catch the light. The effect was perhaps a little too subtle, but given time he assumed it would darken. It would gain definition when dry. Anyway, the signature was what mattered.

That was going to be the hard bit. He'd replied to Merv with a formal letter signed Martin Phelan in the hope that it might elicit a reciprocal response. Instead what had arrived in the post this morning was a letter from Burke's solicitors Dyer & Cummings signed 'Geoffrey Dyer, Senior Partner'. So no joy there. But Merv's handwriting would be a doddle to copy and the pillocks at pAf would never notice. They were that desperate, they'd clutch at straws.

If they didn't go for the one, he'd offer them a twofer.

In the meantime, what? He'd been round to his dad's to sniff the Derain and even to his cauterised nose it still stank of turps. His father had said that varnish would seal in the smell but it was too soon to apply it. The old man had always been a stickler for traditional methods, refusing to use modern driers in the paint. At this rate they'd be lucky if the pictures were ready by next June, let alone this October. The waiting game was driving him nuts. Why hadn't the Post-Impressionists invented acrylics? And that doofus Duval was still refusing to auction the Degas pastel. Him and Dad were as bad as each other.

He turned the Degas nude back to face him. She was on the blowsy side, but a beauty. And she was burning a hole in his bedroom wall when she might have been burning a hole in his pocket.

Chapter XVII

Daniel made it from Finsbury Park to Walthamstow in 10 minutes flat. He raced up the Seven Sisters Road, breezed down Broad Lane, flew over the reservoirs and sped down the Blackhorse Road past St James Street Station. On a sunny Saturday, the pavements around the station were clogged with crowds of shoppers overflowing from the High Street, home of the longest street market in Europe.

Multiethnic Britain. Lithuanian garage, Polski Sklep, Turkish-Cypriot restaurant, dodgy Romanian-run dive named Jack's. Two pubs, both closed, one in the process of being converted into a health club but still empty, with its freshly painted windows gathering grime.

Yasmin lived in an upstairs flat in Ilfracombe Road, a street of Victorian two-up two-downs ending in a park. Most of the houses, originally built for workers' families, had been divided into starter flats for singletons. In Chelsea they would have changed hands for a couple of million; here they went for upwards of £150,000. Some were bijou, with plants in tubs outside. Others had been casualties of the buy-to-let bubble, bought by speculators too skint to spend money on them and let to squabbling families of Polish builders, the ones in work who could afford the rent. The ones who couldn't dossed in the garage lock-ups that lined the dirt track between the back gardens and the railway embankment.

No. 137 was at the bottom on the right, she'd said, just a couple of houses before the park. Halfway down the street Daniel got off his bike. It was hot, the start of a promised barbecue summer and he didn't want to arrive in a muck sweat. Plus his heart was pounding, making him breathless. He wiped his face on his T-shirt, rolled down his right trouser leg and pushed his bike up the street unnecessarily slowly, savouring the pleasure of anticipation.

There were two bells for 137 and no intercom. He rang the top bell and heard the sound of feet running downstairs. Expecting a face to appear in the frosted glass, he jumped when the door suddenly opened apparently unaided.

"Mum's on the phone," said the slip of a boy in the Arsenal shirt standing on the doormat.

Daniel liked the look of Sami. He followed him up.

He found Yasmin curled up on the futon by the living room window, feet tucked underneath her with the sun behind. In jeans and a T-shirt, she could have been Sami's sister.

"Gotta go," she said into the phone, "I've got a meeting. Yes, I *know* it's Saturday, it's not *that* kind of meeting. Tell you later. Love you," she hung up.

"My mum," she rolled her eyes at Daniel, "thinks I work too hard."

She got off the sofa and padded over on bare feet. Her toenails were crimson, her eyes as green as he remembered.

"Cup of tea?"

"Please," he gulped.

"Good of you to come all the way to my 'studio'," she called from the kitchen over the rattle of mugs and the roar of water filling a kettle. "As you can see I'm not really set up for entertaining 'clients'."

A lot of what Yasmin said seemed to be in inverted commas. He hoped that applied to the world 'clients'.

"Sugar?"

"Two please."

"Sami, Mum needs the living room for a while if you don't mind taking the computer into the bedroom."

She handed Daniel a mug stamped with a crown and the logo HMP Wormwood Scrubs.

"He's a computer whiz," she smiled at Sami. "I've bred a geek. Lucky I went into the police, I'll have the right connections to save him from extradition when he's arrested for hacking into the Pentagon."

"He doesn't look like a geek," said Daniel, eyeing the Arsenal shirt.

"Which team do you support?" asked Sami.

Daniel couldn't think of a team, so he said: "Chelsea."

Sami gave him a pitying look and went into his bedroom.

"So, tell me about 'Sheddism'," asked Yasmin over her shoulder as she reached behind the futon and pulled out a large black portfolio.

Daniel explained, and she didn't laugh.

"You've come to the right place," she said. "Walthamstow is a hive of 'Sheddists'. You should see the allotments round the back of the park."

She unzipped the portfolio, laid it out flat on the futon and knelt in front of it, flipping quickly through the plastic sleeves in search of the Nativity. Daniel wished she'd slow down so he could look at the pictures flashing past, as bright and enticing as wrapped sweets on a conveyor belt. He wished the whole morning would slow down indefinitely.

She stopped at the Nativity and pulled it out of its sleeve.

He felt immediate relief – the picture was perfect. Often paintings that looked fine online were rubbish in reality: the colours garish, the handling amateurish. But Yasmin's colours were jewel-like and her touch was assured. From close-up, the Virgin was a brilliant self-portrait. The mop of unruly hair was tucked under a veil but the face was instantly recognisable from the arches of eyebrows, like physiognomic quote marks. And the shed was masterfully rendered, wood knots and all.

"This is really good."

He hoped he didn't sound surprised.

"Can I look at the others?"

He knelt down and flipped through slowly, pausing at each image.

"You're really looking at the pictures!" she said in surprise, looking over his shoulder.

"I'm an art historian. That's what we do."

"Well, these are history as far as the art world's concerned," she said with a half-smile.

"Are you still painting?"

"No…" she indicated the size of the room, and Sami next door.

"I know they're 'miniatures' but where and when would I do it? I'll take it up again when I'm retired… It may surprise you, but I enjoy my job. I like police work. What's the point of painting pictures nobody buys? It's not a nice feeling to know you're wasting your time. I like to feel I'm making a difference."

"But people would buy these."

"Possibly, for insulting sums of money. To be honest, I've had offers but I'd rather keep them. It may sound retentive but they're part of me."

She disappeared back into the kitchen. He heard the fridge opening and closing.

"I'm making me and Sami a bite to eat. Would you like some?"

Chapter XVIII

From the dress code, it might have been a funeral: everyone in the gallery was wearing black. The only way you could tell the caterers from the guests was by their aprons and trays.

The monochrome scheme extended to the art on the walls: large canvases of a uniform washed-out grey all measuring exactly 200x212cm, the off-square format Boegemann invariably worked in. The only variation was in the orientation. Some images were 'portrait', others 'landscape' – the challenge to viewers being to work out which, given the 12cm margin of difference. To mix things up further, the artist almost always painted his figures in 'landscape' format and his landscapes in 'portrait' – except occasionally, to keep people on their toes. "Confounding audience expectations," said the State Gallery's exhibition guide. "Fucking with your mind," said Boegemann.

Not that his paintings could be categorised as portraits or landscapes. His subject matter was global politics, his message that the world as we know it was doomed or, as he put it, "a fuck-up". War, torture, starvation, oppression – these were his themes, although they were not always obvious to the viewer. True, most people could decode the meaning of the big grey balls of the *Barbed Wire* series or the small grey cylinders of the *Land Mine* series. But sometimes his allusions were more elusive, as with the glass of water on the filing cabinet titled *Untitled (Resource Wars)* or the sump titled *Untitled (Black Gold)*.

Brackets were a key component of Boegemann's artistic defence against the world's evils – if he could, he would have framed his pictures between them. Outside the studio, though, he dispensed with them. Dirk was a workaholic, alcoholic, sexaholic, chain-smoking hell-raiser who lived life to the limit. When he wasn't painting he was curating and when he wasn't curating he was networking, and in the short intervals in between he was raising hell.

At 39 he was on the brink of burnout, but he wore his terminal exhaustion like a fashion accessory. It suited him. Without it, his long puffy pasty face might have belonged to a middle-ranking Dutch business executive. With it – and the expensive suit and shirt, worn without a tie but with flashy cufflinks – he looked like somebody. Hell, you'd have to be somebody to look that tired and afford that suit. Most people who looked that shagged-out were dossers.

Dirk's lifestyle would almost certainly have killed him if it hadn't been for his assistant Ernst. Ernst booked the flights, the hotels, the restaurants, the hookers; he ran the studio and he scored the drugs. Some even said he painted the pictures, others implied that if he had they would be more interesting.

Ernst was an artist, or he had been one. Fresh out of art school and scuffling for survival he had landed a dream job with Boegemann that he imagined would advance his career. It didn't advance it, it became it, and Ernst became dependent on the money. Six years on he still seemed fresh out of art school, with that innocent stare in his wide-open blue eyes. If Dirk's face looked lived-in, Ernst's looked like he'd put life on hold and was fast losing hope of ever taking it off.

At this moment Ernst's unblinking gaze was fastened on Martin, who had wangled his way into the reception on Bernice's arm. Ernst had noticed Dirk monitoring Martin's movements over the heads of the crowd of art world A-listers. If he got through this evening without medical assistance, he'd need a pick-me-up later.

Tonight's launch was a big deal for Boegemann; it had

the potential to take him on to the next stage. He'd had solo shows at the Stedelijk in Amsterdam, at SMAK in Ghent and the Schirn Kunsthalle Frankfurt, but his pictures were still only selling for a few hundred thousand pounds. The subject matter was the problem: too depressing, the sort of thing that public galleries could present as educational but private and corporate collectors ran a mile from. He risked being sidelined as a northern European gloom meister unless he could break the transatlantic market, to which this show in London was meant to be a steppingstone. The trouble was that American collectors love colour and indulging their unsophisticated taste would have been a betrayal of everything Boegemann stood for. For the State show, though, he had made a small concession. In the new painting *Untitled (Summary Execution)*, the victim's eye bandage was stained with red.

It wasn't only Boegemann with a lot at stake. The gallery was putting its name on the line by exhibiting a relatively unknown artist without a pre-established media profile in Britain, though the hell-raising, if handled properly, might help. Getting punters through the doors would be a struggle, but visitor numbers could always be faked. Who was going to check? In any case the show was cheap to mount since the majority of the works still belonged to the artist. Most of those credited to a 'private collection' had come straight out of the stores at RazzellDeVere.

The Boegemann show RDV had planned for the autumn was part of a new business strategy of mounting selling exhibitions of contemporary artists. It had worked spectacularly for Westerby's with their one-man auction of works by Cosmas Byrne, but RDV had to fish in shallower waters. With Boegemann they were dipping in a toe. They couldn't have wished for a better shop window than this solo show at the State Gallery. Cassandra Pemberton had a contact in the marketing department who had ensured that all RDV's best clients were on the guest list.

The State's own list included the usual sprinkling of young artists, past nominees and winners of the Ars Nova, whose role was to mingle with the gallery's trustees and patrons rather like hostesses in a Mayfair club. The arrangement suited everyone. It suited the artists to be seen at the State and it suited the patrons to feel they were mixing with artists. If one of the artists occasionally misbehaved it added a faint frisson of excitement, like a dab of eau de bohème behind the ears. It wasn't easy to make the State's clinical white spaces feel bohemian, but a misbehaving artist or two helped. Tonight, though, even Boegemann was behaving. He was off the booze and manfully resisting the allure of the voluptuous redhead in the little black dress, cut dangerously low to expose the red satin trim on her balcony bra.

Apart from the bloodstain on the execution victim's bandage and the odd passing tray of cherry tomato and goat's cheese canapés, the bra was the only splash of colour in the room – until Godfrey's arrival in an International Klein Blue Tie with matching handkerchief in his breast pocket. With Enzo in tow, the collector from Pickton looked ready to party.

Enzo was dressed for the occasion in skinny black jeans and the usual black scoop-neck singlet revealing his nipple rings – not exactly the lounge suit specified on the invitation, though the colour toned in with the funereal crowd. The doorman had been about to refuse him entry when a signal from Jeremy Gaunt, standing by the entrance, persuaded him to let the pair of them through. Instead of showing due appreciation, Godfrey blatantly ignored the paintings – he didn't care for Boegemann – and made a beeline for Martin, who'd finished his business with Ernst and, with Bernice beside him, was staking out the entrance where the canapés came in.

State occasions were never a barrel of laughs, but the party atmosphere tonight was more strained than normal. The Less Important Guests were looking nervous and the VIPs were looking bored. Bernice and Martin seemed to be the only ones enjoying themselves, apart from Tammy Tinker-Stone who had just received news of her nomination for that autumn's Ars Nova.

She was the only British-born candidate on the shortlist – the other three nominees were Tunisian, Lithuanian and Taiwanese.

"She'd better win it for Britain," whispered Bernice to Martin. "She's getting on, and it's her last chance before it goes totally global."

Tammy was on a high, charging around in a black sequined mini-dress and combat boots collecting video footage of her fellow guests for the *Smile Please* project she hoped to have finished by the autumn. Unlike Orlovsky, Gaunt had given her permission to film. The chance of appearing in an Ars Nova video might just add the element of excitement the evening needed.

Tammy's cast list so far included:

Jeremy Gaunt himself and his art historian wife Virginia, an authority on British Modernism. Nigel Vouvray-Jones and his wife Sonya, a cosmetic-surgical work in progress known to staff at RDV as The Old Mistress. Dirk Bougemann and Ernst. Godfrey Wise and Enzo. The museum directors of the Stedelijk, SMAK and the Schirn Kunsthalle Frankfurt. Fay Lacey-Piggott and her Swiss collector husband, Baron Rudolf von Stöckli. The celebrated architects of the unbuilt State extension, Spritzer & Camorra – Spritzer tall, bald and lanky with huge black-rimmed glasses, Camorra small and wiry with a fine head of white hair.

Among the usual smattering of favoured art critics there was the influential Karel Klima from *The Money Paper,* the man responsible for making the reputations of the Cool British Artists – despite looking like he slept in his suit. There was the dapper Tom Jonson, who combined his role as visual arts pundit on *The Culture Programme* with the post of exhibitions director of Orlovsky's London operation. Unlike the adipose Klima he was frighteningly trim and had the unusual distinction, for a thin person under 40, of having already suffered a heart attack from overwork. And of course there was the usual rent-a-crowd of cBas.

Tammy didn't waste any time on them, she could catch up with them later. She avoided Orlovsky too. She knew better than to try filming him, especially with the scowl he was wearing tonight.

Orlovsky was certainly not looking happy. He was hovering near the entrance with a lawyer on one side and a minder on the other – there was no Mrs Orlo in his life – looking as if the decision to come in might commit him to some irreversibly foolish course of action. He was tired and tetchy, fresh off the plane from South Korea and the opening of his newest Asian outpost in the nick of time for the Gwangju Biennale, and this was the last place on earth he wanted to be. He'd offloaded his Boegemanns and regarded the show as an anachronism. In his opinion, this sort of western art was in its death throes. All you could say for it was that it was painting, and collectors never seemed to tire of pictures on walls. This despite the fact that the walls in many of their houses were either made of glass or non-perpendicular, or both.

Who in their right mind would want to wake up to that, he asked himself in front of a bleached-out image of a dusty trainer sticking out of a mine crater? These were museum pictures, and with the museum building boom showing every sign of going bust they were no longer a marketable commodity. A museum artist's prices had to be in seven figures before he was a viable proposition for a dealer like Orlovsky, and most museums didn't have that sort of money. Collectors had money, but they weren't buying this sort of work. No, while the market in 2-D works on canvas persisted, you couldn't beat a Cosmas Byrne dot painting – all style, no content and guaranteed to include a colour that matched your décor. The only problem was getting hold of enough of them since the canny bastard choked off supplies.

The sight of Martin slurping free champagne with Godfrey cranked Orlovsky's irritation up a notch.

"What's he doing here?" he asked his lawyer.

The lawyer pressed a finger against one nostril and sniffed.

Orlovsky followed Martin's movements around the room with the detached assurance of a spider watching a fly.

"Have you sent that letter?"

The lawyer nodded.

"Good."

* * * * * *

Orlovsky excepted, Tammy had got a good haul. All the same, she felt the footage was rather flat and colourless. What she'd really wanted was a shot of Gaunt wringing out one of his tortured smiles, but he wasn't performing. She searched the gathering for him and found him standing with Lady Virginia, Dirk and Ernst beside the big execution painting.

Shit! He was cracking one now and she was too late.

Tammy had caught the State director in the middle of asking Boegemann, in the nicest possible way, if he would consider donating one of his paintings to the gallery at the end of the show. The ingratiating smile had begun its painful progress across his mouth when it was suddenly and unforeseeably stopped in its tracks. From the direction of the Ladies, where she had been fixing her lipstick, the voluptuous redhead had come waggling and clattering over on her platform sandals and, breezing rudely past Lady Virginia, planted a scarlet smacker on Gaunt's crooked puss.

"Shit!" Tammy swore again as an explosion of breaking glass resounded from the other end of the gallery, near the door where the catering staff came in.

Everyone in the gallery turned to look.

Godfrey Wise had apparently collided with a waiter carrying a drinks tray, the tray had emptied its contents onto the floor and Enzo was rolling in the shattered remains.

"Shit, shit, shit!"

Tammy had started filming, but it was too late.

Chapter XIX

The sound of snoring was interrupted by the ringing of a doorbell, but to Martin's surprise when he woke up the snoring didn't stop. He turned around to find a tousled blonde head on the pillow, mouth agape, epiglottis serenading the ceiling.

The doorbell rang again and the snoring faltered but recovered.

Martin rolled out of bed. He knew the score, even in his sleep. Recorded delivery = summons.

Who was it this time? He signed for the envelope and tore it open.

Orlovsky. It couldn't get any worse.

Martin swept the envelope and its contents into the open swing bin and shovelled the week's accumulation of take-out containers on top. He supposed he'd better tidy up for Bernice.

For once he was rattled. Orlovsky spelt serious trouble. He could probably hold Merv off till the Degas ship came in, and he had Duval over a barrel. But Orlovsky wasn't going to hang about. He'd seen the look on his face last night and he hadn't liked it.

How was he going to get hold of that sort of money? Not by selling spunk doodles to pAf, that was for sure, even assuming they were still in the market for them. He'd made them a BOGOF offer last week and he hadn't heard back.

The solicitors' letter that preceded this one into the bin

had estimated the cost of re-landscaping Orlovsky's garden at £500,000. That was 10 times what it cost Martin the first time round, but Orlo didn't know that and Martin wasn't about to tell him.

He snapped the kettle on, rattled the cereal packet, emptied the dregs into a bowl and pulled open the fridge. No milk. Stuffing dry cereal into his mouth with one hand, he made coffee with the other.

Milady would be having her coffee black.

The regularity of the snoring was as reassuring as the ten-second siren at a nuclear plant. As soon as it stopped Bernice would be in there bending his ear with a whole load of blather about last night. That was another of Bernice's faults, too bouncy in the mornings, like a puppy wanting to be taken for a walk.

The snoring had stopped. He heard a toilet flush, followed by a spate of hawking and spitting, and Bernice appeared in the kitchen doorway, wrapped in his bathrobe with an unlit fag hanging off her lip.

"Give us a light Marty love," she growled. Her voice was always deep, deeper in the mornings.

He obliged.

"What's wrong darling? You look like you've seen a ghost!"

He retrieved the summons from the bin, wiped off the ketchup and handed it to her.

She unfolded it gingerly, avoiding the sticky patches.

"Shit, what a bastard. I thought your garden looked lovely, what I saw of it. Honestly, you'd think Orlovsky needed the money... though from what Karel was telling me last night, it's possible he does. There's a rumour going around that he's overstretched. He's opened in five new markets in as many years and they're not delivering the profit margins expected. Plus he's lumbered with old stock he can't get rid of, stuff he paid top dollar for before the recession. He was more heavily invested in the cBas than he likes to admit and the only cBa works surfing the slump right now are Byrne dot paintings, which he's been moaning he can't get enough of."

Martin brightened.

Good, she'd cheered him up.

"I wouldn't worry love, something will turn up. It always does, for a lucky boy like you."

She stubbed out her fag in the cereal bowl, opened the bathrobe and straddled his lap. If she'd had a tail, thought Martin, it would have been wagging.

Chapter XX

Pat had never had much time for Modigliani, a half-arsed dauber in his opinion, the poor man's Cézanne. As far as he was concerned half a Modigliani was as good as a whole one, and half a Modigliani was all he'd got to work from: a black and white photocopy of a reclining nude with the bottom right-hand corner torn away.

As the head was on the top left, everything below the bikini line – hips, bush and thighs – was up for grabs. Pat had some wriggle room this time, and he was planning to enjoy it.

He could have made the pose up out of his head. That might have been Modigliani's way – it certainly looked liked that from his skewed anatomy – but it wasn't Pat's. Pat could conjure an entire apocalypse out of thin air but when it came to the human figure, especially unclothed, the physical intimacy of an actual presence was necessary to him. Caressing the contours of a flesh and blood body with the chalk or brush was what, in Pat's case, produced the magic, and on this flaming late June afternoon in The Shed he was looking forward to caressing some special contours.

Irene's thighs, bless her, were too soft and dimpled for Modigliani. Unlike with the Degas nude, there'd be no disguising the cellulite under a blizzard of chalk. For this particular job he'd asked Suzy to pose, and blow him down if she hadn't accepted.

From what could be seen of Modigliani's model she was reclining in one of the artist's trademark cascading poses, hips twisted out of alignment to face the viewer, sliding down the bed under the force of gravity – the sort of pose a rag doll could comfortably maintain but a human body couldn't endure for more than a minute. Although the tear in the photo was only just below the navel you could tell that things were heading downhill by the steep angle of the right hip in relation to the bed. This was in defiance of the fact that the left hip appeared to be carrying on as normal, following the horizontal axis of the upper torso.

The situation, Pat figured, was that the sex-mad Eyetie had pulled his usual stunt of lying the woman flat on her back, then twisting her hips around to allow the triangle of her bush to peek out invitingly from behind the ellipse of her left thigh. But Pat was a gent. He wouldn't put Suzy through this torture. He could achieve the same effect with the bottom half if the top half was stretched upwards on the diagonal – which, he surmised, was probably how Modigliani did it. That sort of anatomy was a game of two halves.

Modigliani's model had full round breasts, miraculously self-supporting, short wavy black hair and thick black eye-lashes hooding half-closed eyes – about as far as you could get from blonde blue-eyed Suzy, but who would know? He had the top half of the torso already in place, drawn out in burnt umber on the canvas with the flesh tones of the face, arms and breasts roughed in. With the hips and thighs, however, it was all to play for.

Pat whistled as he arranged the drapery on the couch. He'd had to guess the colours, as before, but without the expressive leeway Derain had given him. Earth reds, browns and ochres were Modigliani's staples, relieved by the occasional swathe of blue. Backgrounds were generally dark to throw the flesh tones forward.

Pat had dug out an old army blanket to cover the couch and stuffed the pillow from his bed into a blue case to serve as the cushion under the model's back. He was embarrassed to tell Suzy the painting was a copy, so he'd moved the Seals from their usual spot to the right of the door and backed his easel into the gap, where she wouldn't see the half-sketched image when she came in. What he'd do when the session was over he'd think about later.

In the nick of time he remembered the newly minted Albert Marquet *Pont Saint Michel* propped on a shelf opposite the door, and flipped it around to face the wall.

At the peal of the cowbell, he hurried across the garden at more than his usual speed. Framed in the alley doorway, Suzy looked dazzling in a purple camisole and artfully frayed cut-offs, the green of her dangly glass earrings matching the thongs of her flip-flops and the metallic blue of her toenails matching her eyes. Against the afternoon sun streaming down the alley the fine fuzz on her long brown thighs shimmered like gold.

Pat bottled the urge to carry her over the threshold as a verse of The Song of Songs rose to his lips. With a conscious effort, he bottled that too.

"Where do you want me?" she asked on entering The Shed.

Anywhere, thought Pat. He pointed to the couch.

"If you could lie like this…"

Pat climbed onto the couch and stretched out both his arms, bending them upwards on either side of his head and rolling his face towards her with a sultry expression.

Suzy laughed, a lovely bright tinkle of a laugh. He looked hilarious in his orange shirt with his beer gut bulging over the strap of his belt and his scrawny legs emerging from ex-army shorts to culminate in emerald socks worn with black sports sandals. Dear Old Pat.

He laughed too.

She undressed without fuss and lay down.

Christ almighty!

"Like this?" she asked, raising her arms and bending them back at the elbows.

It wasn't quite like that, but he didn't dare go near her.

"Not quite so bent, the right less than the left. More relaxed, as if they've just fallen into position" – he tried to mime the posture while standing up – "and the head like this." He turned and moued again.

When she laughed a second time, her breasts shook.

Pat was getting an erection.

If it had been Irene he'd have gone over and sorted her out, arranged her limbs as simply as fruit in a bowl, but Suzy he couldn't touch. There was an electromagnetic field around her that if he crossed, he'd be a goner. Anyway the arms didn't matter, they were in already, and the hips – a little thin to go with the breasts in the picture, but never mind – were doing that signature thing, the curve of the topmost thigh causing a partial eclipse of the bush.

And what a bush it was! Moses never saw the like of it. Golden as late autumn, yellow ochre. Suzy was a natural blonde. It felt like blasphemy to paint it black.

Pat had always had a slight tremor in his fingers, it gave a feathery quality to his brushwork that made his paint surfaces quiver. But now when he tried to position the hips on the canvas, his painting hand shook. To steady it, he decided to start by focusing on the left side of the image, the side that was already sketched in. Suzy's breasts were smaller than the Modigliani nude's but it didn't matter, the shadows fell in more or less the right places.

It must be old age; he was losing his touch. He'd never had this trouble with a model before. He had always viewed life painting as a sort of test run: where the brush led, the hand and tongue might naturally follow. But with Suzy he wouldn't have known where to start. A proposition was out of the question: nothing short of a proposal of marriage would do.

By teatime the top half was taking shape but the bottom half was still to do. Pat nipped to the kitchen to make a brew and on his way back across the garden with two mugs of tea – and a couple of bakewell tarts, for a special treat – ran into Suzy, fully clothed, on her way out.

She looked tearful and cross at the same time.

What had he done?

"It isn't *me*," she blurted, "I don't know why you bothered asking. I could have done a better job myself!"

The cowbell tinkled after her like her laughter as the gate slammed shut.

Old fool! He should have started from the other end. Now he was left with half a photograph and half a painting, and they didn't add up to a whole.

Chapter XXI

Everyone wore black, and this time it was a funeral. The collector Godfrey Wise had died, aged 57, and the London art world had turned out in force to pay its respects, even though the ceremony was 200 miles north of the capital at a crematorium on the outskirts of Pickton-on-Tees.

The Wise family had reserved two first class carriages on the 9.05 East Coast train from King's Cross to Darlington, where a coach would be waiting to collect the mourners and drive them the remaining 15 miles to Pickton. Teesdale Cemetery and Crematorium were at the posh end of town, just down the road from the Edwardian villa where the young Godfrey had once disturbed the flies dozing among the forgotten treasures of the Dyce Collection.

Everyone had come. All the seats in both reserved carriages were taken and latecomers who had neglected to RSVP squeezed in among the standard class passengers and paid their own fares. Wise's unexpected death was an event with implications for everyone in the contemporary art world. Dealers, auctioneers, collectors, gallery directors and artists – no one was immune from its effects.

Arts journalists left off the official guest list could always charge their train fares to expenses, but Karel Klima still resented having to sit with a young mother and two small children in standard class while Tom Jonson, wearing his

Orlovsky Gallery hat, was reserved a seat at the top table with Jeremy Gaunt and Nigel Vouvray-Jones.

Marquette's Bernice Stock was not on board. Her last piece on the State Gallery's Boegemann launch had been so bland, after all references to the redhead and Enzo episodes had been edited out by Crispin Finch, that Fay Lacey-Pigott had sent young Daniel Colvin instead.

In the reserved carriages the atmosphere was sombre. There were few tears for Godfrey, generally regarded as a clown. The issue uppermost in everyone's mind was the fate of the collection, the biggest contemporary art collection in Britain and, according to *Marquette*'s last Globalista survey, 7th largest in the world. If it were sold, the market would be swamped.

None of the London crowd had met Mrs Wise. She was said to be a former hairdresser with no interest in contemporary art who left to herself would have collected Jack Vettriano – Britain's most popular artist, unranked by Globalista. The couple's two sons were equally unknown quantities. The younger one, Donald, worked in the family business. The older one, George, had gone into engineering, ran his own consultancy in Newcastle and collected vintage planes.

In the paying seats the mood was more upbeat. The media were on the scent of a good story. What interested the arts journalists and other hangers-on who had come along out of curiosity, like Martin Phelan, were not the consequences of Godfrey's death, which didn't affect them, but the causes of it.

Word was that Godfrey had suffered a heart attack after attending an opening at Orlovsky's with Enzo. The following day, when he failed to turn up for a lunch appointment, the alarm had been raised and he'd been discovered dead in his bed. The results of the autopsy had not yet been made public, but word on the grapevine was that toxicology tests had found a high concentration of methamphetamine in his blood.

Enzo had been questioned by police and released. His story was that he had gone home with Godfrey to the collector's house in St John's Wood, where the couple had argued about his extended visit to the bathroom earlier that evening with a young Scandinavian sound artist, following which Enzo had flounced out.

To those who knew them, the story held water. They were always rowing. And Enzo was manifestly heartbroken. There were no suspicious circumstances, said the police.

Among the art press there was speculation about how much Mrs Wise knew of her husband's London life. Not much, guessed the few who had seen the happy couple together. At home in Pickton Godfrey was the model citizen: a pillar of Pickton Golf & Country Club, twice president of Pickton Rotary Club, a founder member of Pickton Arts Circle and principal patron of the Teesside Youth Inclusion Project.

Though of Jewish extraction – his paternal grandfather's name was Weissman – Godfrey was not a worshipper at Pickton Synagogue. The service in the crematorium chapel would be conducted by a preacher from the Tyneside Humanist Society and the eulogies would be delivered by Marjorie Rimmington, director of pAf, and veteran northern comic Declan Connor, the dead man's oldest friend from primary school.

As the rather shabby crocodile of metropolitan mourners filed along the winding tree-lined walk from the coach park, following the arrows marked 'CHAPEL OF REST', they could just make out a cluster of smartly dressed Picktonians – men in sharp suits, women in heels and hats – at the foot of a grand flight of steps that might have done justice to a minor Egyptian temple.

Against the temple wall to the left of the entrance, like sacrificial offerings, lay heaps of floral tributes in cellophane wrappers and above the wrappers floated a flotsam of hats, bobbing and ducking as their wearers read the messages of condolence. At the foot of the temple steps on the other side a solitary black pork pie hat stood out in tragic isolation, weaving and jerking with the spasms of violent sobbing that repeatedly shook its wearer's fragile frame. Under the hat, the spider-like figure appeared to be dressed in a tailcoat with no shirt.

As the metropolitan crocodile came into view, the gathering on the temple steps turned to look. The VIPs among the Londoners paid no attention; the Less Important Persons looked behind them.

A hearse was advancing slowly through the screen of trees, the bright floral tributes piled on its roof flashing through the foliage as it passed. Mounted on top was a wreath spelling out a message in giant letters.

'FATHER', was it? No, it was two words. 'DEAR DAD'?

It was only when the cortege got clear of the trees that the message became legible: 'OLD MUCKER'.

The mourners stared in disbelief as the hearse drew up and Declan Connor sprang athletically from the leading limo to open the door for his old friend's widow. Shirley Wise stepped daintily out in black patent leather sling-backs, dipping the crow feather fascinator cresting her coiffure, and disappeared up the church steps without looking back. There was no indication of what she thought of Declan's send-off. He stayed behind to take the applause.

The service was mercifully short. The humanist preacher, in a long black Nehru jacket buttoned to the neck, summed up the life of the man he had never known without striking too many discordant notes, although a reference to the deceased's special interest in young people produced a muffled snort from a hack in the back row and a howl from Enzo, who had refused to be seated and was being physically restrained by Orlovsky's minders from running up the aisle and flinging himself on the coffin.

Marjorie Rimmington's address was brief and to the point, a transparent plea to the dead man's family not to call in the Wise Collection loans and leave the town's newly opened gallery empty and its newly appointed director out of a job. Declan Connor's eulogy was longer but more entertaining. His reminiscences of the schoolboy Godfrey running a mobile sweetshop from his satchel, selling half-sucked gobstoppers and hardly-worn licorice laces – one careful owner – at a discount, raised laughter from the family in the front pew and almost made Pickton's Rotarians forgive the wreath. They even succeeded, momentarily, in silencing Enzo.

Odd that he didn't mention the collection, though. To some of the London contingent this seemed ominous – and as would soon become clear, the omens were right.

At the reception in the Captain Cook Function Room of the local Thistle Hotel, Jeremy Gaunt sought out Donald Wise to offer his condolences and express the hope, with a pained smile that was for once appropriate, that he and George would keep up their father's tradition of cultural philanthropy.

Daniel Colvin happened to be standing right behind him when Donald curtly informed the State Gallery director that the Wise family wanted out of the art business as soon as possible. Neither he nor his brother had ever shared their father's enthusiasm; as far as they were concerned his art collection was a load of overpriced tat. Contemporary art was a crazy fad that had cost their father a fortune and ultimately, in their opinion, his life. The family couldn't wait to be shot of it. They'd only invited the London art crowd to the funeral because they were on a list their father, in a premonition of mortality, had drawn up the month before his death. Their mother could keep the Byrne petal painting if she liked; everything else would be auctioned off. He, Donald, couldn't see the point of any of it and George wanted the warehouses for his planes.

* * * * * * *

The mood in the reserved carriages on the return journey to London could only be described as funereal. Despite Gaunt's habitual discretion, news of the threat to the Wise Collection spread through the train like a bad odour through an air conditioning duct. A fire sale of Godfrey's assets was unthinkable. His warehouses were stocked floor-to-ceiling with all the biggest brand names in British art, and if they were all offloaded at once the market would go into meltdown.

Even if the family could be persuaded to sell the collection piecemeal in small lots, observed Vouvray-Jones at the improvised emergency summit convened around Gaunt's table, the storage costs would need to be factored in – and if the Wises wouldn't foot the bill it could fall on the auction houses. It could take years and years of dribbling risk into the market to neutralise the potential fallout from the collection's dispersal, and in the current climate who would want to take a punt on the works' value in, say, 10 years' time?

Godfrey had imported the tat in his discount stores from China, but where art was concerned he had backed Britain. Now, with the developing markets in Indian, Chinese and Middle-Eastern art, the hegemony of the cBas was no longer secure. The situation was fluid enough without a flood of British art being released without warning onto the global market. If you wanted to turn British art investments into toxic assets, this would be the right way to go about it.

For the moment, all agreed that the only course of action was to keep the news out of the media as long as possible while cobbling together a compromise solution.

In his window seat across the aisle from the high table, Bernard Orlovsky was keeping schtum. There was an idea forming in his mind that he needed privacy to pursue. He went to the disabled toilet for space to think, found it engaged and while waiting congratulated himself on not having made Godfrey's parochial mistake of piling exclusively into Cool British Art. As a citizen of the world, he took the global view. Even at the height of Cool Britannia he'd been aware that the ice would eventually melt. He had diversified, kept ahead of the game and now he was simply waiting for the game to catch up. His immediate concern was to keep the Arabs in dot paintings; in a year or two it would be Arabic calligraphy. Liquidity problems were a temporary annoyance, but he wasn't worried. A solution would present itself.

Whoever was in the toilet was taking his time. Orlovsky jabbed impatiently at the door release button, and jumped when the door slid open to reveal Martin Phelan.

The schmuck was everywhere.

"Orlo," Martin greeted him affably with a sniff, "just the person I wanted to speak to. I got your summons and I'm not going to contest it. I'm prepared to settle out of court. Why make extra work for lawyers? They're rich enough."

He noticed his fly was undone and zipped it.

"I don't have the readies right now but I can repay you in kind. I'll call you at the gallery later in the week. Between us I'm sure we can work things out."

Chapter XXII

At 12.30pm on a Monday in mid-August you could be pretty much guaranteed to have The Art Room to yourself. Most of the restaurant's regular patrons would be on holiday and those keeping up the pretence of working were mostly late risers, the type who drifted in for brunch at half-past two. Orlovsky liked a place to be empty when he was doing business, it cleared his mind. And the business occupying it today was especially sensitive.

Though he didn't make a habit of altruism, Orlovsky allowed himself the occasional indulgence. The Wise Collection crisis was not his problem; unlike some others he could name, he had been prepared. It was bound to happen sooner or later, even if Godfrey's death hadn't made it sooner than everyone, himself included, had expected. But while his fellow players were in a state of shock, blinded by their own self-interest, Bernard Orlovsky had come up with a selfless plan that would save the situation for everyone.

He wouldn't make an offer to the Wise family to buy the whole collection in as stock. His altruism didn't stretch that far; he had enough toxic assets of his own. But at least he had managed to stay ahead of the curve.

Global operators of his calibre were men of vision: they created markets, they didn't follow them. For the past five years he had been quietly pruning his holdings of British artists, starting with lightweights like Faith, Burke and Buhler. In their case storage costs were not a factor – Faith's entire oeuvre would fit into an envelope and anyway, Orlovsky wasn't short of space. He had all the room in the world for Cosmas Byrne, a heavyweight on the international circuit whose reputation was by now gold-plated – although recently, it was true, his diffusion lines had been selling better than the big set pieces in museum vitrines. There was a limit to the number of vitrines the museums of the world could accommodate. When every museum had one, what then? Building more museums had once been the answer but now, in the place of museums, there were holes in the ground.

That wasn't his problem either, fortunately. But no one was immune to a major upset that undermined investor confidence in the market. At a time when confidence was already weakening and high net worth individuals who would once have invested in golden calves in museum vitrines were putting their loose change into gold ingots, a clearance sale of the biggest contemporary art collection in Britain could be catastrophic.

Back in the day when the teenage Bernie was flogging end-of-roll fabrics on 39th Street, clearance was the standard fix for liquidity issues, but what worked in the schmatte trade didn't work in the art trade, for several reasons. One, with the sums involved you'd drop millions. Two, you'd betray the clients who'd bought from you at inflated prices and destroy their confidence in your judgment. Three, you'd screw the market for everyone else, which might be a plus in other areas of business but was a minus in art. In a market where prices were professionally inflated, consumer confidence depended on them staying that way. One or two burst balloons you could get away with; a whole bunch of them and the party was over.

From his usual window table overlooking Albemarle Street, Orlovsky watched Jeremy Gaunt step out of a taxi and tip the driver with that contortion of the lips that passed with the poor death's-head for a smile.

The dealer grinned broadly to himself, as he knew how, and tightened his tie. In a way, he felt sorry for Gaunt. He suspected a loveless childhood locked away in one of those British correctional youth facilities called public schools. He wasn't anticipating a convivial lunch.

True to expectation, the meal got off to a sticky start. Orlovsky ordered white Burgundy with his sea trout; Gaunt asked for Badois water with his vegetarian tartiflette. Neither spared a glance for the art on the walls which was the restaurant's chief selling point to other customers. What was pleasure for other diners was business for them.

They talked about the Dubai Art Fair, the rising price of Middle Eastern art, the new class of contemporary collectors in China. When Orlovsky finally introduced the subject of the Wise Collection over coffee, he approached it crabwise. He was a master of the oblique attack.

"When your extension's built, what will you fill it with?"

Gaunt met the surprise question with a bleaker smile than usual, conscious that Orlovsky wouldn't swallow the official media line trotted out by the State Gallery that the new space would be filled with unhung works from the stores. The dealer knew what the stores contained. So he deployed his own tried and tested tactic for fielding unwelcome questions, which was to answer one with another.

"What would *you* fill it with?"

"The Wise Collection."

"The Wise Collection," repeated Gaunt, taking off his glasses. "How?"

"Simple. By acquiring it."

Without wishing to remind Orlovsky that he was speaking to a man whose office overlooked a £150m funding hole, Gaunt found himself asking the obvious question: "What with?"

The waiter interrupted with a brandy for Orlovsky and a plate of petit fours. Gaunt usually refused sweet things with an air of pained asceticism, but before he noticed he'd eaten two of the biscuits and picked up a third. They were rather good.

"I'll tell you what with," Orlo leaned on both elbows across the table. "I'm getting old. I'm overweight. I've got heart problems, which this stuff"– he tapped the brandy balloon – "isn't helping. I've got no family apart from my old mother and no one to leave the business to when I die. Godfrey may not have had impeccable taste, but the sheer breadth of his collection is unparalleled. It's an extraordinary record of the history of British art at the turn of the 21st century. It would be a tragedy for it to be dispersed; it belongs in a museum. If I had the time and energy, I'd open my own. But why go to the trouble and expense when there are more than enough contemporary art museums in this country already – none of them, of course, with the stature of the State.

"If you want the Wise Collection, it's yours. I'll donate it to the gallery on one condition: that the gift is anonymous. I don't want people thinking I'm a philanthropist, I'd have every schnorrer in the country after me. This would be a one-off benefaction. I'd like the donation to be attributed to the Wise family. I don't foresee any problems with that."

The dealer was now beaming from ear to ear as he reached across the table and laid a large fuzzy hand on the director's arm. It was as much as Gaunt could do not to retract it.

"That's an extraordinarily generous offer," he gulped, without even attempting a smile.

He needed to think quickly. There was the obvious problem of where to put the collection if, God forbid, the extension was never built. An image was forming in his mind of a line of dump trucks emptying the contents of the Wise Buys warehouses into the crater outside his window, when a workable alternative suddenly suggested itself. The storage problem could be relieved by lending works to other galleries. Whole exhibitions of works from the Wise Collection could be sent off on tour around the regions, solving the programming problems of regional galleries built in the boom years with nothing to fill them. At the same time, national tours of the Wise Collection could be used to spread the contemporary art gospel outside London. If some of the art was already passé, who was going to notice? Audiences in the regions were decades behind.

He managed a smile. "I'll need to discuss it with the trustees."

Orlovsky capped the smile with a broader one. "Of course. But remember the gift is from the Wise family." And to his lunch companion's acute mortification, he winked just as the waiter arrived with the bill.

Before they got up from the table, Gaunt was committed to launching the new exhibition galleries in the State extension with a survey show of the Russian contemporary artists who, as it happened, were even now filling the space in Orlovsky's stores vacated by the British.

Chapter XXIII

The twelve 7ft square canvases only just fitted through The Shed door, and when stacked inside they left no room for the paint. The deliverymen had dumped it on a pallet on the veranda: twelve 5-litre cans of household gloss in different colours and four of ultra white acrylic polymer.

Pat stood and stared at it. It couldn't stay there. If it wasn't gone by the time Ron came home from work he'd never hear the end of it.

He put out a Mayday call to Dino, who promised to come over with a tarp. If they cleared the brambles between The Shed and his other neighbour's garden, Dino would be able to bodge a temporary storage facility.

Individual copies were one thing, this was another. Ever since Marty could squawk his demands had escalated. Pat could wave goodbye to The Seven Seals until this was over. If the Blue Orangers didn't bash out this batch of canvases pronto, the bastard things could be clogging up the works for weeks.

Typical of Marty to spring this on him just when he was on the brink of a major breakthrough in the Seal department. Artists shouldn't have children. They competed for attention, and in Martin's case it never stopped. Celibacy was the only answer really, or it would be if it weren't for women.

Pat was still feeling sheepish about Suzy. He'd almost

thrown in the towel when the Modigliani went pear-shaped, and now this.

Dot paintings, Marty called them. Love hearts without the love, as far as Pat was concerned. Making one-off copies had been just about bearable, but now Marty seemed to be moving into the wholesale business. His collector friend was apparently developing a luxury hotel and wanted one of these paintings for each of its 'Imperial Suites'. Sweets for the suites, each one a little different. Different? With grids of 6in dots at 6in intervals, as different as a bunch of paint charts to Pat.

It wasn't as if Pat even needed the dosh. What he'd got for the Derain alone would pay Moira's rent for a year. But Marty was in some sort of financial trouble, and when your flesh-and-blood is in a hole you have to dig them out. Plus some of the Blue Orangers could use the money. Dino was behind with the rent again and had been asking Pat if he could doss in The Shed if his landlady followed through on her threat to evict him.

Pat had never been one to spoil the party. He'd present it to the class as a colour exercise though, to be honest, the idea made him queasy. It was a little thing and it might sound stupid, but the step down from copyist to hotel decorator felt degrading.

He felt more positive after Dino pitched up with a tarp and a barrow full of skip wood and, latterday Palladio that he was, knocked up an all-weather lean-to in 15 minutes flat. The paint cans were safely stashed and the two of them were propping up the bar of the Hook & Mackerel before Ron had even boarded the bus from work.

"Drinks on me tonight," said Pat, "Happy Hour extended until closing. You're a *salvatore*!" he added in his best Italian, rolling the 'r' around his mouth as he raised his first pint.

"*Salute*," answered Dino, raising his. "How did you know Salvatore was my middle name?"

By closing time their joint diplomatic decision to alternate Irish whiskey chasers with sambuca had improved their command of each other's languages beyond recognition, the deterioration in pronunciation only serving to enhance their mutual understanding.

At a certain point in the evening it dawned on Pat – or was it Dino? – that he was in a position to make conditions. He'd make it a condition of signing on Marty's dotted line that his collector friend invested in Pat Phelans – small ones for the tiddlers, big ones for the biggies. If he could build a hotel with all those sweets for dots he could build a church with a chapel for each Seal.

Pat fell asleep that night with love hearts dancing before his eyes, saying: "ANGEL FACE… SUGAR LIPS… CUDDLE ME… JUST SAY NO".

Chapter XXIV

It was Crispin Finch who broke the story on the cover of September's *Marquette*:

'POUND SHOP BILLIONAIRE DONATES £150m COLLECTION TO STATE GALLERY'.

"With the British art world rocked by news of the sudden death of the UK's most prolific contemporary art collector, Godfrey Wise," Finch's scoop began, "*Marquette* can disclose that the family of the deceased has entered negotiations to donate the entire collection – presently held in Wise's birth-place and business base of Pickton-on-Tees – to the State Gallery. A public announcement has yet to be made, but Sir Jeremy Gaunt is said to be overwhelmed by the family's generosity.

"Speculation remains about where the collection, currently occupying three hangar-sized warehouses on the outskirts of Pickton, will be housed – or indeed shown – before the long-awaited completion of the State Gallery's new wing. But a gallery source has told this magazine that one plan under consideration is for the collection to tour the UK in a rolling programme of regional gallery exhibitions.

"The broadcaster and curator Tom Jonson has welcomed the news. 'Londoncentrism is the curse of our culture indus-try, nowhere more so than in the field of cutting-edge art,' he told *Marquette*. 'It is one of the nation's ugly secrets. The Wise family's generosity may help to widen the circle of contemporary art to embrace the regions, giving them equal access to the sort of challenging work previously only seen in the capital. In his earlier loans to the Pickton Art Foundation Godfrey Wise pioneered a model of good practice which, with the resources of his collection at the State's disposal, could be rolled out across the country from Penzance to Orkney. With the addition of the Wise Collection to the nation's holdings, cutting-edge art can become truly national'."

There was no mention in *Marquette* of the circumstances of the collector's death, which received widespread coverage in the tabloids. *The Daily Star* ran with the headline 'PILL-POPPING BILLIONAIRE ART PUNTER POPS HIS CLOGS', while *The Sun* led with a picture of Enzo on the steps of Teesdale Crematorium Chapel captioned: 'Dead collector's pierced punk lover in floods at funeral'. Neither article made any reference to the donation.

For once the tabloids had stuck to the facts, thought Daniel; it was *Marquette* that had gone out on a limb. From what he knew the donation story was a fabrication, but no one at the magazine had deigned to consult him. Miffed at Daniel being sent on the funeral jolly while Fay had him chained to his desk churning out last-minute copy to fill the gaps left by reneging advertisers, Crispin had refused to even bring up the subject.

As far as he was concerned, Daniel was too junior to have an opinion. So Daniel kept schtum and watched with mild amusement as Crispin primped and preened around the office about his scoop. The day after publication his story had been taken up by *The Times* and *The Independent*. There was a lead feature on page 3 of *The Telegraph* on Tuesday and *The Guardian* was obviously planning something, as their arts correspondent had just rung for a quote.

To Daniel it made absolutely no sense. He'd heard Wise's son and heir with his own ears effectively telling Gaunt to take a running jump and now the family had apparently changed their minds. Why the sudden volte-face? It didn't figure. He had a vivid recollection of the look on Donald Wise's face when he gave the State director the bum's rush. No, it simply wasn't possible.

Yet Crispin's source at the State was bound to be reliable. The gallery had obviously got its hands on the collection. How? If it wasn't a gift it had to be an acquisition, and that cost money. Whose? Not the State Gallery's, that was for sure, since £150m just happened to be the precise sum the gallery was still struggling to raise to finish its extension. So where had the money come from? And why the secrecy?

Something funny was going on and Daniel wanted to find out what, if only to wipe the misplaced smile off Crispin's face. But who was going to tell him? He hadn't a hope of getting a peep out of Gaunt and from his brief acquaintance with Wise boys he didn't fancy his chances with them either. The weakest link, he reckoned, was the mother.

The key to the mystery lay under that big hairdo. From Mrs Wise, thought Daniel, he might get the truth.

Chapter XXV

Laid out in pairs, the dozen canvases covered the back garden of 15 The Mall with a narrow margin for manoeuvre between them.

To get them to lie flat Dino had mowed the lawn. The patch of grass and weeds between the kitchen and The Shed had never previously merited the description 'lawn' – Pat preferred to think of it as a wildflower meadow – but Ron had been muttering about the state of it for years, and Pat had now called his bluff and borrowed his Flymo.

As luck would have it, a band of high pressure was settled over London and the dry spell was forecast to continue for the next fortnight. Long enough to get this lot out of this way, but what a criminal waste of outdoor painting weather.

That was what Pat needed right now, a blast of plein air, a late summer outing for the pochade box. Maisie had told him about a place in Walthamstow where her brother had an allotment and had promised to take him there before the summer was out. A day out painting with Maisie was just what the doctor ordered, as reviving to the spirit as a visit to a spa. All this copying was making him constipated; he needed a spot of creative irrigation.

From the kitchen where he was making breakfast for himself and Dino, the grid of white canvases reminded Pat of Ruisdael's bleaching fields. The way the morning sun was printing shadows from the overhanging pear tree on their pristine surfaces seemed to compound the offence of covering them in dots. It had taken Pat and Dino days to prepare them, applying the white ground, then plotting out and drawing circles for the dots. Dino was rubbish with a brush but he was ace with a compass. The trouble with the compass was it left holes.

Anyone would have thought they were running a playgroup. For the past week they'd been collecting yogurt pots and polystyrene egg boxes for mixing and holding colours. The mixing would be the creative bit, so far as it went, and in that department Pat was giving the Blue Orangers a free hand. He didn't want to deprive them of their only fun. He'd confine himself to the role of nursery assistant.

When the class arrived, to his surprise and secret disappointment they took to the 'exercise' like ducks to water. The morning passed in a happy burble of background banter that Pat would normally have clamped down on, but what did it matter? Wolf's pox doctor joke even got a laugh from Yolande. Pat let it go. On a normal day he would have imposed silence so that the class could listen to the colours, but all the colours were saying today was 'rhubarb, rhubarb'. There was no synaesthetic sensation involved; it was just a case of dots before the eyes.

Still, further into the session Pat was forced to admit that the results surpassed his expectations. By mid-morning some distinct colour trends were emerging: the first faint glimmerings of an expressive range. When Marty had given them carte blanche with the colours he had had no idea what the Blue Orangers were capable of. Pat felt proud of his class; he'd trained them well. They had learned something about colour after all. As the dots spread out from the centre of each canvas, the paintings were taking on individual moods.

Suzy's was bright and breezy, as expected: clear greens, blues, yellows and pinks, matching the spangled toenails she was sporting this morning. Judging by the insouciant dangle of this morning's earrings – multicoloured bunches of Murano glass fruits – she seemed to have forgiven him the Modigliani.

Wolf, who had warned that once he got onto his knees he'd never get off them, had propped his canvas up against The Shed veranda and was applying unmixed red, yellow and blue in circles radiating outwards from the centre. He had complained loudly about the absence of black paint, but they were under strict instruction not to use it – the one instruction that they had been given. Without black, Wolf had to resist the temptation to paint a drop-shadow under every dot.

Yolande, true to form, was the only one causing trouble on account of her congenital resistance to colour. Pat had never quite worked out what she was doing in his class. In the first half-hour she'd used up her stock of grey and was demanding more, which Pat refused to give her. Her response was to tip all the other colours in her egg box into one yogurt pot and add white to mix different shades of sludge. Viewed from the far end of the garden, the tonal impression produced by her canvas reminded Pat, in a funny way, of Ben-day dots from a blown-up photograph of a footballer's knee.

Grant, freed at last from the unwelcome distraction of a subject, was in his element arranging orange, red and brown dots in repeating patterns, while Maisie, bless her, had picked a perfumed bouquet of shell pinks, aquamarines and lilacs and was scattering them like petals over the canvas. Pat breathed in their fragrance audibly as he passed, making her laugh. She was doing well, the old girl, on her hands and knees, a veteran of the doorstep-scrubbing generation.

Dino, predictably, was having difficulty staying inside the lines, but Pat said nothing – he'd tidy up after him with a bit of white later. If they kept up this pace and got through six this morning, then weather permitting they'd be shot of the whole lot next week.

Fast work this painting and decorating business, you could say that for it. Catching a glimpse of The Seals through the open Shed door, Pat whistled 'We'll meet again' under his breath.

Things were looking up.

At break time he brought out a tray of tea and biscuits: Fox's Party Rings from the discount rack at the local Londis, only two days past their sell-by and they looked festive.

Wolf got a laugh by grabbing a handful and laying them out on Maisie's unfilled dots while Pat was in The Shed fetching her a chair. When the old girl finally got to her feet, she revealed a pair of pastel-coloured knees, one green, one pink.

"You wouldn't say that I'm no oil painting, would you?"

Maisie had made a joke. Everyone laughed, including Pat.

Chapter XXVI

Shirley Wise lay on the emperor bed at the hub of a grey-scale wheel of fine woven wool suits in a range of charcoal, steel, donkey, dove and pearl.

Godfrey had always fancied himself in grey. He liked to think it gave him a touch of Italian chic, or 'chick' as he persisted in pronouncing it even after people corrected him. Godfrey enjoyed mispronouncing foreign words, it was one of his things.

If she was going to do it she'd have to do it now or the suits would hang in the wardrobe forever and before too long the wardrobe would become a shrine.

The suits, at least, the Age Concern shop would be thankful for. They'd turned down the ties – a bit on the bright side, the lady said, not to everyone's taste. And there were other things at the back of Godfrey's sock drawer they wouldn't have greeted with enthusiasm, things made of bits of string and leather that Shirley couldn't work out where they went, and didn't want to. She had picked them up with the tips of two frosted fingernails and dropped them in the bathroom bin like so many shrivelled banana skins.

Poor Godfrey.

She blamed herself for not noticing. It seemed the whole world had known about it, just not her. But how could she have guessed that the man she married, the fit young sporty type smiling out of the wedding photograph on the chest of drawers, was going to turn the corner in middle age? A sportsman, a grafter, a family man. She'd heard some stories in her day – she was a hairdresser – but nothing like this.

You could live with someone for 30 years and never really know them. It was the art that started it, the art and the parties. Godfrey had always been a party animal. The suits she'd miss, the art she wouldn't. Left to herself she'd give it all away, if anyone would take it. But that wouldn't be fair to George and Donald. It was worth money.

There was a discreet knock on the bedroom door and a Filipino face appeared around it.

"There's someone to see you, ma'am, a young man called Daniel. He says he's got an appointment."

Shirley had quite forgotten.

"Oh yes Juanita, tell him I'll be a minute."

That would be the reporter from *Hair & Beauty* magazine, come to interview her about the Hair Raising Brunches she had been organising for the Hair & Beauty Benevolent Association in aid of children with alopecia. Shirley was an HBBA bigwig; she had set up the charity's North East branch.

She put down the pearl grey suit she was holding, picked up a styling comb from the dressing table and expertly inserted the steel end into her bouffant. Standards must be kept up: high hair, high spirits.

She sighed to herself and went downstairs.

The reporter was standing in front of the fireplace in the living room studying the Cosmas Byrne petal painting above the mantel.

For a lad from a salon magazine he looked a bit scruffy, but that's what the trade was like these days even at the top. That so-called stylist to the stars Nicky Clarke always looked like he'd been pulled through a hedge backwards. If you looked past the haircut, or lack of it, the lad had an honest face. She'd been dreading the interview and had thought of putting it off but actually, when it came to it, it was a welcome distraction.

With his glasses, his serious expression and his reporter's pad the young man reminded her of Clark Kent, though for someone from an industry magazine she was surprised at how little he seemed to know about the HBBA. Still, it was a subject she could natter on about forever and seeing him scribbling notes was rather flattering. She wasn't used to people hanging on her words. She was almost disappointed when the questions stopped and he closed his notebook and stood up.

"I'm very sorry about your husband," he said politely.

She'd been right about him, he was a nice young man.

"What are you going to do with his art collection?" He was looking up admiringly at the petal painting. The question took her aback, but he explained: "I went to art school before going into journalism. Art's my pet subject."

"Between you and me and the gatepost," she lowered her voice, "we're going to sell it. Art was my husband's passion but none of the family share it. There's a dealer down in London who's agreed to take the lot off our hands – except for that," she indicated the petals, "that I'm hanging onto."

"Which dealer?" Daniel had to ask.

She looked put out by the question.

"I'm not the right person to ask. My sons could tell you. Some foreign bloke with a name like the Russian mafia. They're all a mafia, that lot, aren't they?"

"You're not wrong," said Daniel, smiling. "Thank you for your time. It's been a pleasure talking to you."

* * * * * * *

Orlovsky. It had to be. But why? Why would Orlovsky want to buy the Wise Collection anonymously and then give it away without taking the credit? It was being touted as worth £150m, but even if it was worth a third of that it made no sense. Plus, although he wasn't exactly short of stock you'd have expected him to cream off the best pieces first. And if he had decided to donate it to the State, lock stock and barrel, why not in his name? He was not averse to publicity.

The trolley service came by and Daniel bought a cup of tea and a flapjack. He was tingling with nervous excitement bordering on terror. He had a feeling he was sitting on an IED of a story that if he wasn't careful could blow up in his face.

If it *was* Orlovsky, it needed expert handling. Who could he talk to? No one at *Marquette*; Crispin would have him crucified. And he had to confirm that it *was* Orlovsky. He sensed that he was already way out of his depth and might soon be too far out to swim back to shore. He needed advice from a professional.

He pulled out his phone and texted Yasmin.

When the phone rang an instant later it made him jump, earning a scowl from the woman opposite. It was the Quiet Coach.

He took it into the vestibule before answering.

"DC Desai here," came a teasing voice. "How can I help?"

Chapter XXVII

The fine weather had held until the weekend. From halfway down Ilfracombe Road Daniel could distinguish a small Arsenal-red figure doing keepy-uppies at the end of the street.

"Hiyah," Sami acknowledged him without pausing. "Mum's upstairs."

A sash window flew up, a curly head popped out and a bunch of keys came flying down.

"Here, catch!"

Daniel locked his bike to a railing and let himself in.

Yasmin was at the door of the flat in an Indian print sundress, one strap escaping over her shoulder. She was wearing flip-flops. He'd never seen her legs.

"I've promised Sami a picnic in the park. I know it's not the height of professionalism, but would you mind if our meeting took place on a rug?"

She shook out a tartan blanket and folded it into a bag, then picked up her dark glasses off the hall table.

"Better enjoy the sunshine while it lasts. The person who misses his chance and the monkey who misses his branch both cannot be saved, as my nan used to say. Indian proverb."

She picked up the bag and slung it over her shoulder.

"Coming?"

Daniel had his reporter's pad in his hand. It was too big fit in his pocket and he felt stupid taking it to the park, so he left it on the table and followed her downstairs.

"…39," counted Sami as they came out.

Daniel noticed the ball was autographed.

"Mum's boss gave it to me, he's got a gold season ticket to the Arsenal," boasted Sami, running ahead with the prize possession tucked under his arm.

The park was oddly empty for a sunny Saturday, but it wasn't exactly bursting with attractions. It was a flat, featureless rectangle framed by poplars where in Magritte's dreams it might have rained bowler-hatted men from a blue sky. Beyond it, Yasmin said, lay Shropshire Fields Allotments, a Shangri-La of sheds of all shapes and sizes in varying stages of romantic dereliction. On any other day Daniel would have made a beeline for it, but today he was perfectly happy staying put.

They spread the rug under one of the poplars and Yasmin emptied the bag's contents onto it: sandwiches, crisps, apples, Kit Kats and cans of drink.

Sami started on the crisps.

"Tuna?" Yasmin offered Daniel a sandwich and took one herself. "OK, I'm ready to take questions. Fire away."

"You've read the piece about the Wise Collection in this month's *Marquette*?"

Daniel wished he could read her reactions through her dark glasses.

"I read the opening paragraph," Yasmin confessed. "We have a subscription in the office, but months go by when we don't get round to taking off the cellophane wrapper. And with all due respect to the quality of its reporting," she handed Sami a sandwich, "I don't have time to read it at home. All I know is that the collector Godfrey Wise has died, in shady circumstances" – the arc of one eyebrow showed above one dark lens – "and his family have dumped the collection on the State Gallery. Anything wrong with that?"

"Nothing in principle," said Daniel, "but in practice plenty." And he described how he'd been standing behind Jeremy

Gaunt at the collector's funeral when the State Gallery director was informed by Donald Wise in no uncertain terms that the family planned to flog off the whole collection.

"And from the look on his face, he wasn't kidding."

"Possibly not", Yasmin helped herself to an egg and cress sandwich, "but they could have changed their minds. Grief does funny things to people. And the manner of his death and his relationship with that young artist Rico…"

"Enzo," corrected Daniel.

"…Enzo might have clouded their judgment. They'd be crazy to put the whole lot up for auction at once, it would cause an immediate collapse in prices. They'd lose money on the deal themselves and it would be disastrous for the market as a whole."

It was Daniel's turn to raise an eyebrow, two in fact.

"Precisely."

Sami's hand was inching towards a second crisp packet when Yasmin deftly replaced it with an egg and cress sandwich. She sat in silence for a moment pondering.

"What was the source of the story about the donation? Where did it come from?"

"*Marquette*'s chief reporter Crispin Finch got it initially from one of his contacts at the State Gallery, and a press release followed. There's no doubt that the collection is headed their way, they're making plans to tour it around the country. That was what the press release was about."

"So if the Wises haven't donated it, who has?"

"Orlovsky?" Daniel phrased it as a question.

"You must be joking! On what evidence?"

"13…14…15…" Sami had gone back to his keepy-uppies.

Daniel described his meeting with Shirley Wise and her remark about the Russian mafia. "What other London dealers can you think of with Russian-sounding names?"

Yasmin thought for a second and answered: "None. Precisely."

Daniel laughed. "If it *is* Orlovsky, the big question is why?

He's not known for his philanthropy. The collection is valued at £150m."

"I think you've got your answer."

Yasmin's glasses had slipped down her nose and her green eyes were regarding him closely over the top.

"What?" he asked, aware of sounding stupid.

"The collection is valued at £150m."

Daniel stared. He couldn't see where this was going.

"My guess is it's worth nothing approaching that. On the open market it might go for £30m."

"So Orlovsky's ridden in like a knight in shining armour to rescue the market? It doesn't figure. Everyone knows he's getting out of British art and going global, he's made no secret of it."

"The market is the market," said Yasmin.

"Another Indian proverb?"

She blanked the question and offered him the choice of an apple or a Kit Kat. He chose the apple.

"33...34...35...36," came from Sami, who'd marked the Kit Kat for later but wasn't stopping.

"It's a question of confidence, or con-fidence, depending how you look at it. Orlovsky created the market in Cool British Art. If the people who bought it from him as an investment (and let's face it, how many bought it because they liked it?) realise they've been sold a pup they'll take their custom elsewhere. 'The one burnt by hot milk drinks even cold buttermilk with precaution.' Yes, it's an Indian proverb, before you ask."

"But why the gift to the State Gallery?"

"That's an interesting one." She pushed her glasses back up her nose and thought for a moment. "Kit Kat?"

Daniel declined.

Yasmin bit into an apple. "If Orlovsky bought the whole collection, he'd have problems. In the current climate – apart from a few choice pieces like the Byrne petal painting – it could take years to shift. Storage isn't cheap and it's money down the drain if stock is losing value. Unlike the Wises, Orlovsky's not in the warehouse business."

She took another bite.

"In any case it would be sending out the wrong message. Orlovsky's made it plain that his attention is shifting eastwards; that's where the thrust of his marketing strategy will be directed. Reinvesting now in British art would throw that strategy into reverse and do serious damage to its credibility. A hundred and fifty million isn't an awful lot to Orlovsky, even if he pays full whack – which you can bet he hasn't, as he's got the family over a barrel. Plus he may be banking on return favours from the State. A public gallery in a commercial dealer's pocket is like a goose that lays golden eggs and stamps each one with its personal seal of approval."

If that wasn't an Indian proverb, thought Daniel, they must come naturally.

Yasmin tossed her apple core behind her into the bushes, covered a yawn and stretched out on the rug.

"How's that for an explanation?" she looked up at him with her hands behind her head and her feet crossed.

Pretty damn good, he had to admit.

"Is it legal?"

"Probably. Many dodgy-looking transactions in the art market are. The Wises transfer the whole lot to Orlovsky by private treaty sale and he gifts it anonymously to the State. What's wrong with that? There's nothing illegal about anonymous donations. For Orlovsky making the collection over to the State could carry big tax advantages, the bigger the more he exaggerates the collection's value. And then, of course, there are the money-laundering possibilities presented by a private treaty transaction… But you don't want to go there. That's an investigation for Interpol, not for a gonzo arts journalist with a thing about sheds."

She took off her glasses, lay back and closed her eyes.

"62… 63…64…65" counted Sami.

"How can I find out if it's really him?"

"Ask him."

Yasmin meant it as a joke, but Daniel's mind was already running through possible pretexts for an interview.

"And now, if you don't mind, it's siesta time. I usually grab one after lunch under my desk, but a tree is nicer."

"70!" yelled Sami. "A record!"

Yasmin opened one eye, smiled at him, and closed it.

"Come on," said Daniel. "Mum's resting. Let's see how good you are against a live opponent."

"Mind that ball," murmured Yasmin, "it's a collector's item."

* * * * * * * * *

It was only later, on his way home to Finsbury Park, that Daniel remembered the pad. He got off his bike to text Yasmin but she'd beaten him to it.

"Got your notepad. Text your address and I'll post it. Btw I thought you were an arts journalist, what's with the hairdressing? Pardon my curiosity, professional interest."

"Don't post it," Daniel texted back. "I'll pick it up when I come back to visit the allotments. I can explain about the hairdressing, honest, Inspector."

Chapter XXVIII

Since Ron Wilkins started as a cashier at the Muswell Hill branch of what was still, in 1988, the Nationwide Anglia Building Society he had only missed two days' work. One was in 1996 when the upstairs neighbour's boiler burst and flooded his kitchen and the other was the day of his mother's funeral.

Two years ago almost to the day that was: 3rd of September, God rest her soul. But yesterday afternoon at work his jaw had started aching and he'd begun feeling hot and queasy. He'd got home alright, not felt like dinner – though he usually looked forward to his Wednesday night chilli con carne – and had gone to bed.

At 5am he'd woken with a splitting headache, swollen glands and a raging sore throat. He found his mum's old mercury thermometer in the bathroom cabinet and took his temperature. It registered 103! When he rang the NHS Direct telephone service they diagnosed mumps and told him to stay home until he was better. The nurse on the other end of the line advised him to take Paracetamol, drink plenty of water and apply a cold compress to the swelling. Bed rest was the only treatment for the disease, but if his temperature didn't go down he should call his doctor. He should avoid going out for the next five days, as the disease was highly contagious. Apparently there'd been a spike in cases in London caused by the arrival of unvaccinated immigrants from outside the EU.

Just his luck, thought Ron, running a mental scan of all the swarthy-looking individuals he'd sat next to over the past week on the bus to and from work. The exercise made his temperature rise. So it was thanks to immigrants coming here to take our jobs that he'd had to call in sick for the first time in his working life, thanks to foreigners importing their filthy germs without a visa that he was here on a Friday morning sweating under a duvet on the living room couch with a sockful of ice around his neck and another sockful melting in the bucket beside him.

'Bed rest' was for skivers, an admission of defeat. At least on the couch he could look out over the garden. He'd got nothing to read, having forgotten, in the state he was in yesterday evening, to pick up his free copy of the *Evening Standard*. Ron never bought the papers, couldn't see the point of paying good money for news you could get for nothing. Some evenings he only did the cryptic crossword.

He'd never been much of a reader, never acquired the habit. Novels, to his mind, were a complete waste of time. Fiction was for wimps and women. The only publications on his shelves were military histories and an almost complete run of back issues of *Making History* magazine dating from his period as Treasurer of the Medieval Combat Re-enactment Society. That was before his historic bout of hand-to-hand combat with the Society's President, an idiot who needed a calculator to count. Ron still didn't know what all the fuss had been about. The man was asking to have his head cleft with an axe and Ron had only given it a light tap.

There wasn't anything worth listening to on Radio 4. The news came round without variation. Nothing happened on a weekday when you were off work. Ron dozed on the couch, drifting in and out of consciousness, until the dum-dee-dum-dee-dum-dee-dum reveille of *The Archers'* theme woke him. He'd missed it yesterday evening and the thought of the 2pm repeat put lead in his pencil. He picked the lukewarm sock off his neck, dropped it in the bucket and got off the couch with a splitting head to put the kettle on.

The kettle stood on the kitchen windowsill overlooking the garden, and flicking it on always caused a surge of irritation at the sight of the enormity of his neighbour's shed. He was sure the old hippy never got planning permission, if he even knew such a thing existed. Ron would have had it taken down by the Council if it hadn't replaced the wilderness of brambles and bindweed that previously scrambled over the hedge and smothered his clematis. And since it went up, the family of foxes that used to sun themselves on Ron's lawn like they owned the place had pushed off and taken their flea-bitten brood elsewhere. He regarded the foxes as Phelan's responsibility: refugees who had taken asylum in the slum of his garden. Ron resented his own garden being invaded by nature. There was still a yellow stain where the foxes lay which no amount of Miracle-Gro Patch Magic would fix.

Just recently, though, Phelan's shed had been expanding. Only last Saturday, while having breakfast, he'd noticed that a bulge had appeared on the far side like a boil in the night. God alone knew what the old hippy used the place for. He never saw anyone coming or going.

Until now, that was.

As he squeezed the teabag against the side of the mug and popped in two NutraSweets, Ron's peripheral vision picked up movement in his neighbour's garden. He looked up to see the shed door standing open and Phelan framed in the entrance with a large square canvas almost as tall as the doorway, which he was carefully manoeuvring through the opening into the arms of a man on the deck outside. Ron thought he caught a flash of polka dots as the swarthy-looking individual – probably the carrier of some foreign disease – covered the canvas in bubble wrap from an industrial-sized roll and passed it down the steps to someone below.

At this point the canvas vanished below the line of the hedge, which was 10ft tall on his neighbour's unclipped side.

Ron watched Phelan reappear with a second, a third and then a fourth dotted canvas, each one duly wrapped and swallowed from view. With wobbly legs he climbed onto the kitchen chair and then the table, affording him a clear view over the hedge.

On Phelan's back lawn a chain of handlers – two men and two women – were passing canvases down the garden and into the side alley between the houses, where an elderly lady with a shopping trolley was wheeling them away. Ron counted 12 out of the shed before Phelan shut the door and disappeared with the Dago and the others down the alley.

With a spurt of energy Ron scrambled off the table and scuttled to the front room window overlooking the street, where a white hire van was parked with its back doors open. On the tail lift stood that delinquent son of Phelan's, loading the canvases into the van. When the last one was in, he pulled out a wad of cash and counted out notes – big red £50 smack-ers – to the four handlers, the trolley lady and the Dago, while his father stood on the pavement watching. Then he closed the back of the van, jumped into the cab and was waved off by the group on the pavement.

So that was it. Caught red-handed. Phelan was running an unlicensed factory from his shed, turning out canvases for cash on the black economy. For the past week or so Ron had suspected someone was sleeping there, as the light seemed to be on at all hours. Now the truth was out. His neighbour was operating as an unlicensed gang-master. That lady with a shopping trolley was clearly a pensioner and there was an older gentleman walking with a stick.

Ron found the number of the Planning Department. He felt a whole lot better, though his balls hurt.

Chapter XXIX

Shropshire Fields Allotments lived up to their billing. In the slanted light of an Indian summer afternoon, they glowed. A grande allée of rough cut grass ran down the middle of a vast expanse of autumnal vegetable patches, crisscrossed by rows of overgrown bean canes, bolted lettuces, mildewed marrows, wilted maize stalks and burned out sunflowers. As Yasmin had promised, the place was alive with sheds.

It was veritable shed heaven. There were sheds of every conceivable design that could be constructed from clapboard, plywood, fibreboard, corrugated plastic, corrugated iron, discarded doors, discarded windows, bits of old mirror – any material that would keep water out – with roofs swathed in scaffold netting or smothered in vines. It was a free-for-all, with no distinctions of class or school. Arte Povera shacks cobbled together from plastic sacking, polythene sheeting and soggy hardboard stood alongside model Appalachian log cabins; mini-Merzbarns mingled with Gothic follies.

The posher the shed, Daniel noticed, the poorer the vegetables. The posh sheds apparently functioned as landlocked beach huts complete with deckchairs, tables, even parasols. An elderly couple was having tea outside their prefab model, a Wendy house for her, a Walden for him – a sop to atavistic urges no amount of civilization could quash. A less salubrious establishment two plots down appeared to be in fulltime occupation, the return to nature semi-permanent to judge from the build-up of cider cans and vodka bottles outside. A tea towel pinned to the window twitched as Daniel passed.

Shropshire Fields was evidently more than shed heaven; it was shed hell and purgatory too. That explained the crucified scarecrow and the tortured gloves mounted on broom handles, apostrophising the heavens. Too scary for bird-scarers.

Daniel snapped away with his camera, as happy as a pap at a premiere. Everywhere he turned he found visual echoes, here of the rickety stable in Hieronymus Bosch's *Adoration of the Magi,* there of the weird wooden structures of Philip Guston, who as a boy of ten had found his father hanged in the garden shed.

Out of courtesy he refrained from photographing allotments whose owners were at work, though on a midweek afternoon there were very few. At the end of the *grande allée* on the right he spotted a shed in a delicate shade of sun-bleached blue as luminous as the sky in Piero della Francesca's *Baptism of Christ*. He was about to take a picture when he became aware of a couple sitting in its shade.

The woman wore a flowery lilac dress and the man a bright orange shirt and camo shorts. Daniel wondered how he could have missed them: they must have blended into the bed of dahlias and Michaelmas daisies behind. It was only when the man cleared his throat in a commanding manner, like an actor launching into a soliloquy, that Daniel noticed them.

This couple weren't drinking tea; they were busy painting. The man had a pochade box in his lap and the woman had a small canvas apparently lashed to the handle of a shopping trolley.

Sunday painters out on a weekday. Daniel suppressed a patronising smile as he crept up behind them to sneak a look.

The woman's canvas was a blizzard of soft marks, an inchoate haze from which vague forms were emerging. Sweet peas? There were sweet peas growing in the next allotment, but it was still a little hard to say. The pastel palette seemed too delicate for dahlias and too pink for daisies, though Daniel had to admit the painting had promise. The brushwork breathed.

The man's was a sketch of a shed, and what a sketch it was. The shed in question was a common-or-garden model two plots down: clapboard, single window, felted roof, Wickes standard circa 1980. Apart from the faint romance of its faded green paint it was unprepossessing, one of the least interesting structures Daniel had seen. But the door was ajar and through it you could see the wheel of an upturned barrow, the edge of a red-striped deckchair and the diagonal handle of a garden fork leaning up against a cobwebby window.

As a subject it was nothing special. It would not have occurred to Daniel to photograph it and if he had, people would have wondered why. But on the small scrap of board in the man's pochade box the contents of that shed, caught in slanting sunlight, were exposed in an intimate moment of revelation as tender as the unlocking of a heart. What colour were the shadows? Daniel could not have named them. They were as warm and rich as coagulated blood.

Just then the woman noticed Daniel and tapped the man's arm.

"We've got an audience," she whispered, and smiled shily.

Daniel felt himself blush as he apologised for disturbing them.

"That's beautiful," he pointed at the man's painting.

"Yes, it's a prince among sheds," the man replied. He waved his brush-holding arm around the allotments. "This is a necropolis of princely tombs, the Royal Cemetery of Ur, E17. A garden of remembrance," he declaimed in a voice as rich and resonant as his throat-clearing.

The woman smiled again, this time at Daniel.

Daniel itched to photograph the picture but it seemed intrusive. Instead he heard himself asking if he could buy it.

"I don't suppose so. It comes with the allotment," answered the man, indicating its surroundings with fluttering hands.

"Not the shed," laughed Daniel, embarrassed. "I meant the painting."

He hadn't even considered what it might cost.

"Oh, that."

The man looked a little shocked, even defensive.

"It's not finished," he said with an air of finality.

"Can I photograph it then?" Daniel persevered.

"If you like," said the man and turned the lid of the box to face the camera, striking an authorial pose behind it. It was about as close to a swagger pose as could be achieved in a folding chair with a wooden box in one's lap.

The woman looked on indulgently, and laughed.

"Now, if you don't mind," the man told Daniel, "we've got work to do. The magic hour will be over in another 10 minutes. Tempus fugit."

And he turned the box back around and picked up his brush.

Daniel thanked him and left. He wanted to ask his name but felt he'd already intruded enough. Still, on his way back he sneaked a photo of the two of them sitting painting, with the shed with the open door behind. For some reason he could not have identified, he wanted to fix the moment in his memory.

* * * * * * *

It was ten to seven when he rang Yasmin's bell; she'd said she would be home after 6.30. His heart leapt as he heard footsteps running downstairs, then sank as the door flew open and he saw his notepad in her hand.

She apologised for not inviting him in. Sami was ill, the doctor had diagnosed mumps and she wouldn't want to ruin Daniel's prospects.

Daniel was touched by her concern for his prospects, but it didn't lessen his disappointment at being sent away. He wished Sami a swift recovery and thanked her for the tip about the allotments.

"I've spent the whole afternoon there and only just scratched the surface. I'll be back."

She handed him the pad with an apologetic smile.

"Did you get anything on Orlovsky?"

"Not yet, but I've arranged to meet him next week on the pretext of an interview about the global pandemic of dot painting exhibitions he's planning for his various outlets in the autumn. I hear it's going to be called *Dot dot dot*."

Yasmin didn't laugh. She looked taken aback.

"I hope you know what you're doing. This isn't hairdressing, you know – Orlovsky is a gangster. These days he can afford to keep his hands clean, but there are some things daily manicures don't change. Other people do his dirty work for him." There was a hint of reproof in her tone as she added: "Take care," and closed the door.

Chapter XXX

It was 90 degrees in the shade in the harbour at Collioure and freezing everywhere else. An electric heater was fanning hot air onto the fishing boats and the fishermen loafing on the waterfront, but it couldn't disperse the damp in the rest of the basement.

Autumn had come early. It had been chucking it down since the middle of September and the buckets in Duval's conservatory needed constant attention. The central heating timer in the kitchen upstairs was set to come on when his wife returned from work, and he was no longer permitted access to it. But why bother with heating? There was no possibility of receiving clients in his 'basement-showroom', which looked more like a junk shop than an art dealership since Valerie had had all his possessions carted downstairs.

Duval's office now contained an 18th century French armoire, the green leather chesterfield Valerie had always hated – she accused it of turning the drawing room into a gentleman's club – and the baby Bechstein grand. The rowing machine was under a polythene sheet in the conservatory beside the stacks of cardboard boxes with soggy bottoms holding his record collection and overflow art library, which had previously enjoyed the run of the house. The shelves upstairs had been evacuated in advance of the divorce because, said Valerie, she needed to take in lodgers.

Now every remaining cranny was filling up with unsalable pictures by Pat Phelan. So far Duval had managed to squeeze them in behind the piano, but the pictures kept arriving and getting bigger. If this went on they'd have to take their chances in the conservatory with the rowing machine. Still no sign of the Modigliani, never mind the Jawlensky and the Vlaminck. And on completion of those, Martin had warned, his father was threatening delivery of a series of seven-footers.

Artists! The most deluded race on earth. They imagined that all that was needed was a gallery where their work could be seen and the world would immediately beat a path to their door. Poor fools! That was only the start of their painful awakening. The gallery was where it all began to go wrong.

In the privacy of their studios artists could dream that the pictures they were painting were revelatory, that their vision would flick a switch in the viewer's mind that would illuminate the world in a new light. But in the glare of the gallery they woke up to the fact of public indifference. You could count on the fingers of one hand the private views where people actually looked at the pictures. If anyone did, it was an odds-on bet that they were fellow artists. Everyone else, even the critics and collectors, stood with their backs to the pictures and drinks in their hands.

The buzz at a private view rarely reflected the quality of the art. It was a measure of the artist's fame or notoriety, and there was no chance of acquiring either of those assets over the age of 35. If you hadn't impinged on the public consciousness by that age you were finished, at least until you were good and dead. There was nothing more a gallery could do for you.

Of course Duval hadn't said anything to Martin. At this stage in the proceedings they couldn't afford further delays. The rest of the pictures would have to be ready for the February auction and the timing was tight. To be honest, in the present state of his finances it was becoming a struggle even to scrape together the necessary to pay Pat Phelan his paltry £3,000 a shot. What was keeping Duval going was the thought of the October auction and the quantitative easing it would bring.

He picked the Derain off the easel and sniffed it. Getting there. He'd take it in for Nigel to look at next week. There was still the faintest whiff of linseed about it, but he'd wear after-shave. If God was merciful he'd give Nigel a cold.

Duval sat down at the piano and lifted the lid. He'd been playing it a lot since it had been down here. Over the music stand he could see a row of Phelans, a series of the Thames around Rotherhithe painted while the docklands were in the throes of redevelopment. He stood up, took down the one on the end and turned it over, as dealers do, to look at the back. The words 'Iron Parthenon' were scribbled on it.

The Parthenon in question was a trio of iron columns supporting the remains of a ruined jetty. It had a Piranesian grandeur about it, towering blackly above the disintegrating hull of an old Thames barge beneath. You could only distinguish the water by the misty V-shape carved between the near and far bank of the river, where the angle of a crane rose through the fog. The paint-handling was tremulous, the touch was tender but the drawing had a grasp of iron. There was something about the little picture, a certain feeling, a sense of life quivering in the shadows.

Duval knew how many years of squinting at colour it took an artist to breathe life into shadows. Yet in the shadows this picture would remain.

He propped it on the music stand, sat in front of it and picked out the opening bars of a Chopin nocturne. The yellow sky above the blackened Parthenon was a tangled mass of jagged, swooping strokes that shrieked abandonment like seagulls' cries. There was nothing he could do with the Phelans, but they suited his mood.

Chapter XXXI

Orlovsky prowled up and down the line of dot paintings leaning against the walls of his Islington office like a tiger eyeing visitors through the bars of its cage and deciding which of them to have for breakfast.

"Imodium, Strepsil, Bazuka, Lemsip, Fisherman's Friend…" he snarled into the speakerphone transmitter, "where's the invention, the mystique in that? You can't even come up with a decent title. Parma Violets? They went out in the 1950s. What did you do, go through your grandma's bathroom cabinet?"

There was a crackly silence at the other end.

"Your artists haven't grasped the basic requirement: anonymity. You shouldn't be able to tell one painting from another. These paintings are as different as chalk and cheese, or…" he flapped his arms in search of a better analogy, "smarties and sugared almonds. The point is," he scowled at a grid of orange and brown dots propped alongside a pastel study in pinks and mauves, "all the colours should be different *within* each picture. The colourways shouldn't differ from each another," he slipped involuntarily into textile terminology, "although each painting should be subtly unique so that the viewer is challenged to spot the difference. The random nature of the colour selection is what gives the works universality. They go with any décor.

"Did you buy remaindered paints, or what?"

Trust the schmuck to economise even on that.

"I provided the artists with the full range of paints," Martin Phelan's voice came over the speaker. "I was told to give them a free hand and these are the shades they chose."

"And another thing," Orlovsky pulled open a drawer of his desk and got out an eyeglass, "the finish is shoddy."

He bent over a painting and scanned its surface.

"All your dots have compass holes in the middle. Cosmas would never let a painting leave his studio in this state. He cares about workmanship. That's the key to his success, attention to finish. Billionaires don't buy paintings with holes in."

"They buy Lucio Fontana," offered Martin. "In the context of medication you could see the holes as twinges of pain."

There was a knock and the shaven bullet head of one of Orlovsky's minders appeared around the door.

"Listen sunshine, it's more than a twinge of pain you'll be feeling if you don't get this load of crap out of here by tomorrow morning. And by the way, when you're ready, my lawyers would appreciate a response to their letter."

The minder cracked a smile as Orlovsky cut the speaker.

"Daniel Colvin to see you."

"Who? Oh yes, the reporter from *Marquette*. Send him in."

Orlovsky swiveled his office chair away from the dots as the minder returned with the reporter in tow.

"This shouldn't take long," Daniel smiled. "I know how busy you are."

Orlovsky didn't smile in reply. He noticed his visitor studying the dot paintings with curiosity and wished he had moved them. Too late to worry about that now. What did a young kid like him know anyway? He looked fresh out of college. They should have sent a senior reporter, like Crispin Finch.

The minder gestured Daniel to a chair but didn't leave. He stood behind him looking at the rows of dots with what was, for him, unusual interest. Funny, he was thinking, if you screwed up your eyes the dots in the one on the left made a shape like a goalie's legs performing a diving save.

When he unscrewed his eyes he found Orlovsky's glaring at him. He shifted his focus to the back of Daniel's neck.

"I can give you 10 minutes," said Orlovsky, pulling up his shirt cuff to expose the face of his Patek Philippe. "Shoot."

The reporter started with all the obvious questions. Why this moment for a global dot painting retrospective? Was it the last gasp for a series that Byrne had warned he would be discontinuing in a couple of years? What was the explanation of the works' international success? Had there been any development in the paintings? Again, Orlovsky saw him looking around the walls. Did Byrne have a new diffusion line in the pipeline?

Between each question Orlovsky consulted his watch. The cub reporter was wasting his time. He could have found all of this out from the press release, if he'd bothered to read it.

"Is Byrne the only one of his generation you think will last?" was the kid's next question.

"If I'm honest, yes," was the dealer's reply.

"Then why are you buying the Wise Collection?"

The question hit the dealer smack between the eyes.

The minder stiffened and shifted his gaze to Daniel's ears, which were turning pink.

"Buying the Wise Collection? Are you crazy? Wherever did you get that preposterous idea?"

"From Godfrey Wise's widow, at the weekend."

For the first time in the interview Orlovsky looked at Daniel, assessing his capability like a firearm.

"Then all I can say is that the old girl has lost it. Grief will do that to a woman, especially after the shock and embarrassment of her husband's death. You should have spoken to the Wise boys, they're the ones in charge. Call yourself a journalist? Do some proper research."

He nodded at the minder.

"Now, if you don't mind, you've wasted enough of my time. Tell Fay next time she wants an interview not to send an intern straight out of journalism school."

The minder pulled back Daniel's seat and took his elbow with a vice-like grip to escort him out.

Orlovsky watched them go.

He'd handled it badly. He shouldn't have let himself get rattled, but it had come out of nowhere. He might live to regret his involvement with the Wise Collection. That's what you got for generous impulses; they should be resisted.

How much did the kid know? Not much, he suspected. What he certainly didn't know – and only Orlovsky's accountant was aware of – was that the dealer had borrowed money to buy the collection against the promise of a Russian exhibition at State.

There were influential business interests in Russia who felt strongly that Russian contemporary art was undervalued by the west. In fact these interests felt so strongly about it that they took the undervaluation as a personal affront. As things stood, Russian-speakers were still responsible for 90% of investment in Russian contemporary artists, a situation that was going to have to change if the market was ever going to take off. Sales of work by Russian artists in London auction houses the previous year had represented less than 2% of the total. Unless the Russians broke into the British and American markets, their prices would never get off the ground.

There was work to be done, and Orlovsky was ideally placed to do it. He had helped his Russian friends in the past with a spot of laundry and they were ready to help him in return. Everything now hung on the State Gallery show. If the show derailed, his backers would be disappointed and they didn't handle disappointment well.

Chapter XXXII

By 7pm the preview for RDV's Boegemann sale would be in full swing, but Fay Lacey Piggott – the woman known in the trade as Network Southeast for her dedication to social linkage – was still at her desk. The joke was unfair on Fay, who was a lot more punctual, although tonight she'd be missing the speeches and perhaps, in these times of austerity, even the champagne.

To be perfectly honest, she wasn't that bothered. She'd seen it all where Boegemann was concerned – there were only so many shades of grey a girl could take – and any VIPs who turned up to this evening's reception would have been at the State exhibition a few months before.

Been there, done that. So the little black dress she had collected from the dry cleaners that morning was still hanging on the back of her office door, its plastic cover bloating in the air from the fan heater she had switched on against the autumn chill.

Outside Fay's office window it was spitting with rain. Inside, the editor's mouse scurried over the face of her hot pink Marilyn mouse mat, whiskers twitching with unusual nervous excitement.

She'd been right about Daniel. This was dynamite. Suddenly it all made sense; the story held water. But could *Marquette* run it? That was the question.

The loss to advertising revenues was difficult to predict. Things were bad enough in that department already; they could hardly get worse. Orlovsky had friends, but he also had enemies. And personally speaking, there were no loyalty issues. Orlovsky had always politely ignored Fay; he was funny with women. He preferred to deal with Crispin. That's how funny he was.

One thing for sure, the revelation wouldn't improve relations with the State Gallery, although no shame attached to their acceptance of a gift in good faith. In the current climate, rather the reverse. In the middle of an arts funding crisis a public gallery could only be congratulated on a massive saving to its acquisitions budget.

The advantages, Fay reckoned, outweighed the risks. If they broke the story in the next edition of *Marquette*, it would be front-page news in the following day's papers. It was the sort of scoop a niche magazine editor dreams of. And for a flagging circulation it would be a shot in the arm.

The mag went to press the day after tomorrow, but it was doable. She'd get the article lawyered first thing in the morning.

Fay prided herself on a talent for quick decisions that she'd always felt was wasted in her job. Things would need to be shifted around. She consulted the flat plan. If she spiked Crispin's page 8 story on the burgeoning Russian art market – of which she'd seen precious little evidence – and moved the page 1 feature on the proposed modifications to the State extension to page 8, she could clear the front page.

The Russian art market piece could wait. If it was burgeoning, it was certainly taking its time. The story could run next month, or the month after. Next year, even.

Daniel had left early for a meeting with his thesis supervisor but Crispin was still skulking around the office, working late on a piece about Orlovsky's global dot fest headed 'Around the World in Eighty Dots'. Crispin was crap at headings, but she'd change it later. 'Dot dot dot...' was better. She'd email him her decision about Daniel's article and attach a copy. She couldn't suppress a smirk at the thought of poor old Crispin's face when he read it. All the same, she'd rather not stick around to see it.

She snapped off the heater, slipped into the little black dress and, holding her framboise Louboutin platform pumps in one hand and her umbrella in the other, let herself noiselessly out of the office. Ten past seven. If she found a taxi she might just make it to the reception before the gannets finished off the canapés. She hadn't realised how hungry she was.

Stepping gingerly out from the shelter of the porch onto the wet pavement, she wished she'd worn her flats and spared her Louboutins. Too late, she wasn't going back in for them now. She would face Crispin's hangdog features in the morning.

Fay pinged open her umbrella. The City had shut up shop. The street was empty except for a white transit van parked with its hazard warning lights flashing on a double yellow at the junction with Cordwainer's Lane. The van had a logo of a speeding picture frame on cartoon wheels with the slogan 'You've Been Framed' inside it.

Funny. Fay wondered idly what a framer's van was doing in the City at this hour. The two men in the driver's cab were consulting something. GPS, she imagined, they must be lost. As she leaned out over the kerb to peer behind the van for approaching taxis, she thought she saw the driver look up at the lit windows of *Marquette*'s office on the 4th floor. It seemed a little curious but right at this moment, with the rain pissing down, her immediate concern was her framboise Louboutins.

At last, a taxi with its light on. She flagged it down with her open umbrella and clambered in.

From his 4th floor window Crispin watched the black cab swallow the rain-splattered raspberry heels and sloosh around the corner. He clicked 'forward' on the email with the attachment, added Orlovsky's personal address and hit 'send'.

Chapter XXXIII

It was the smell that struck him first as unfamiliar, the mingled scent of sanitising gel and roses. When he opened his eyes the light was painfully bright. He didn't remember having strip lighting at home.

A curtain was pulled back and a face loomed over him. An attractive face, young, female, in designer glasses, but one he couldn't put a name to.

"So, you're awake! Welcome back to the world of the living. I'm Ashraf, the junior house doctor on your ward. You're in the Whittington. You had a lucky escape."

That explained the smell. He seemed to be in hospital.

"What happened?"

"They brought you in last night with concussion and a broken leg. Traffic accident in Finsbury Park, hit-and-run driver. A police officer is coming in later to take a statement. The paramedic said your bike was spaghetti hoops. You were lucky to get away with a broken leg."

She checked his pulse and scribbled on a clipboard.

"CAT scans clear – no brain damage, but I'd go easy on the Sudoku for now."

Daniel stared at her. How did she know all this stuff about him? She'd even sussed his Sudoku habit.

His head felt like a pumpkin; he remembered nothing. He reached a hand under the sheet and hit plaster just below his groin. It was his left leg, then.

"Broken below the knee, compound fracture. I wouldn't book the skiing holiday just yet. If all goes well the long cast will come off in a month or two and you can be fitted with a casual knee-high model. But I wouldn't start saving for a new bike yet. I recommend public transport, if you value your life."

A new aroma blended with the gel and flowers as the food trolley rolled past. "No dinner for you until tomorrow," said Ashraf cheerily, clipping his chart to the bedrail and vanishing.

Daniel hoisted himself on his elbows and pulled up the pillows behind him. There was a control for adjusting the bed but he didn't dare touch it; he felt too fragile and accident-prone. In the end the dinner lady came to his rescue. He wanted to thank her, but the stink of her trolley was making him nauseous. It was only when she had wheeled it away that he located the source of the scent of roses: a big bunch of yellow blooms with an envelope on the bedside cabinet.

He opened the envelope and pulled out a card.

"To my star reporter. Come back soon, can't manage without you! xx Fay."

Kisses, and an exclamation mark? From Fay?

Like water seeping through cracks, it began to leak back. His piece on the Wise Collection. Fay had liked it. He felt relief, self-congratulation even. But that didn't explain the broken leg. Or did it?

To his fragmented consciousness they seemed connected.

He'd left work early on the excuse of seeing his tutor, not wanting to be there when the shit hit the fan. As far as he remembered he'd gone straight home to Finsbury Park. After that, a blank.

He was on his bike. Going where? Oh yes, to Lidl's. He'd been on his bike going to Lidl's to stock up because the fridge was empty.

What then?

He lay back on the pillows and stared in front of him. There was a print of Van Gogh sunflowers on the wall opposite, the one from Munich with the aquamarine background, and he thought how cheap and nasty it looked in its plain white frame. Funny, wasn't it, how even the pioneers of modern art needed old-fashioned gilt frames to look imposing?

Suddenly he saw it. Crossing the junction between Seven Sisters and Blackstock Road, being splashed by drivers going past, then the picture frame on the side of the van and the impact.

There was something written inside the frame.

What was it?

A nurse popped her head around the curtain.

"There's a police inspector to see you."

It was Yasmin, in that snappy blue suit.

"How did you know I was here?"

It seemed incredible when he'd only just found out himself.

"I've been ringing your mobile since yesterday afternoon and getting a 'number unavailable' message. I wanted to ask you how the meeting went with Orlovsky and when I couldn't get through I started worrying. I had an awful feeling something had happened, and when I called your office and they told me you hadn't come in, I did a missing person check around the A&Es.

"I've notified your boss. Tell me what happened."

Chapter XXXIV

Artists were like dogs, thought Pat, they needed taking out for a sniff around or they pined. Yesterday's outing to Shropshire Fields had done him the world of good. He'd bounced out of bed this morning with his tail wagging and his ears pricked.

The effect on the Seals had been spectacular. Last night's session on the Fifth had been a real humdinger; he had finally wrestled The Souls of the Slain to the ground. For years they had been haunted by the ghost of El Greco, but last night's final push had sent the spook of Toledo packing. So confident was Pat of victory, in fact, that he hadn't tucked the picture in for the night. He wanted it up and ready to greet him in the morning.

A few more nights like that and The Seals could be winging their way to the purpose-built chapel of Pat's imagination, three down each aisle and the seventh over the altar.

Holding back on the cobalt violet had been the answer. Pat recognised his weakness for the colour. In his chromology violet was the colour of love, hence the temptation to go overboard with it. But last night he had resisted its blandishments. He had even left a mound of it on his palette under cling film, in case it came in handy for this morning's Jawlensky.

It was a measure of how chipper Pat was feeling that the thought of this morning's copying couldn't dampen his spirits. It was the very last that he'd agreed to do, and he was ending on a high note. Alexej von Jawlensky was an artist he could get along with, a man after his own heart. A Russian aristocrat, a man of the spirit, a painter who could make his colours *sing* – not just expressionist *con brio*, but expressionist *con amore*.

The still life subject made it easier. It meant he'd have something to paint from, something that wouldn't storm out in a pet while he was making tea complaining that he hadn't done it justice. Jawlensky had always insisted on something to paint from, he didn't make things up. He wasn't a synthetist, he was a synaesthetist. What looked like a bowl of apples to Gauguin sounded to Alexej like the music of the spheres.

The composition was a twofer: portrait format with a compotier of fruit in the foreground and a vase of flowers behind. The flowers hung over the fruit in the compotier like a mother bending over her brood to check they were leaving for school correctly dressed. Scrubbed, combed and pomaded. The apples of her eye.

Pat had already plotted the colours. Cobalt blue for the compotier and vase, the family connection. Greens, pinks and yellows for the fruit, with one violet plum almost – but not quite – plumb in the middle. Alexej specialized in off-centre compositions. If you drew a vertical line through the middle of this picture, the vase and compotier would be performing a pole dance around it.

The fruits in the photograph were different shapes and sizes, while Pat's were all apples scrumped from the same tree. No matter, it was similar enough to see how the light fell. And the fact that the flowers were fabric didn't matter either. Nothing you couldn't fix with a brush and paint.

He whistled as he crossed the lawn with a big black boom box, another recent acquisition from Maisie's shop. Jawlensky called for music and he had just the thing, a red CD embossed with a gold hammer and sickle: *The Best of the Red Army Choir*. True, Alexej left Russia before the Revolution and his army service was with the Imperial Guard, but why quibble over details? The red of the Red Army Choir ran in his veins.

The Fifth Seal greeted Pat warmly on entry, and he reciprocated with a friendly salute. Nothing to fear in that department; he could rest easy. The Jawlensky still life was ready and waiting with the composition sketched out on the prepared board in indigo paint and the black and white photo tucked into the easel rest.

Something you could never judge from a photograph was scale, but as the Russian tended to work relatively small Pat had cut the board to 20x30cm. It was an old piece of mount board from a charity shop painting he had picked up chez Maisie, dated 1963. Out by few decades, but who was counting? A blink in the eye of eternity.

Pat shifted the easel over to the left to get the Fifth Seal out of his line of sight. He was happy for the picture to hum to itself in private, but he didn't want it interrupting. If there was going to be background noise it would be coming from the Red Army.

He picked up the photo and squinted at it. There was a darkness in the tone of the tabletop that seemed to come up from below, like rising damp. He'd start with indigo and go over later in a lighter colour. Magenta, maybe. That should strike a warm bass note for the tenor voices of the blue crocks to rise above. Further warmth, he thought, might be extracted from a backing chorus of raw sienna on the wall behind, dusted with orange like a smoggy sunrise. Jawlensky's signature strategy of weaving horizontal and vertical brushstrokes would allow the fabric of the picture to breathe.

Propped on the shelf behind the easel Pat could see the Vlaminck and the Marquet, signed and sealed and awaiting delivery. He moved them out of his line of sight to a position above the Fifth Seal, along with the book of signatures Martin had lent him, which he'd sworn on his honour not to cover in paint.

The International Directory of Artists' Monograms and Indiscernible Signatures, 1800-1991 by John Castagno, published by Scarecrow: the name of the publisher tickled him, as did the 'indiscernible'. He couldn't see what difference a signature would make, but the collector was apparently a stickler for detail. Funny what collectors minded about: everything but the painting, really. Marquet's signature was firm and neat, Vlaminck's was a scrawl. He'd had a reasonable stab at them. They were discernible. Who was going to notice anyway?

The Red Army Choir was belting out *Kalinka* as he blocked in the fruit; when their voices modulated into the tender strains of *The Nightingales* he feathered in the roses. When they broke into *The Troika's Gallop* he turned up the volume while he mixed a deep, deep green from terre verte and ultramarine for the densely shadowed foliage at the heart of the picture – which was why he didn't hear the cowbell.

* * * * * * * * * *

From the complainant's description, it was not quite what Planning Enforcement Officer Hank Dooberry had been led to expect. Still, in his experience you should never judge a house from its front. What went on round the back of people's houses was nobody's business – except of course the local planning department's.

There was nothing remotely business-like about the frontage of 15 The Mall, though if you were running an illegal business you'd be stupid to advertise it. You'd be astonished what people in the London Borough of Haringey got up to in innocent-looking sheds in their back gardens. Breeding pit bull terriers and growing cannabis were the least of it. They'd found a shed last year round the back of a terrace in Green Lanes that was being run as a massage parlour by illegal Bulgarian immigrants. That was a major violation, it made the BBC News. A painting factory, whatever that was, sounded relatively minor, but every complaint had to be followed up.

Well this lot weren't exactly hiding anything. There it was, a big carved wooden sign on the alley door with the words 'THE SHED' daubed in large white letters over the name

'SEA VIEW'. He searched for a bell, tried the door handle, which came off in his hand, and spotted a toilet chain hanging from an ironwork bracket with a ceramic toggle reading 'PULL'.

He pulled, and heard the distant clang of bells.

Nothing happened.

He pulled again, twice, and went round to try the front entrance. There were three bell pushes, none apparently connected, and a big brass knocker – a pair of knockers, you might say – in the shape of a mermaid.

He lifted the siren politely by her tail and was just about to bring her down with wallop on the scallop-shaped plate when he heard a loud "Halloo" from the alley.

"Come out, Invisible Man, wherever you are!"

The voice was so resonant it made him jump. He tripped backwards down the step and dusted off his dignity by producing his ID card.

"Hank Dooberry, Haringey Planning Department. We've received a complaint about a temporary structure at the back of this residential premises being used for a commercial purpose. Are you the householder?"

"The Shedholder," said the man, "Pat Phelan," and held out his hand.

Dooberry looked him over. His clothes were as peculiar as his tradesmen's entrance – red flowered shirt worn over a yellow t-shirt with grey camo pants and sandals over emerald green socks. His hair could have been described as camo-coloured too. Dooberry would have been pushed to identify its shade, which ranged from silvery red at the roots to black at the tips. When the man bent down to reattach the door handle, the back of his head made Dooberry think of Davy Crockett's hat.

"I expect you'd like a look," the man cleared his throat with a theatrical flourish. "You'd better come through."

As he led the way down the side alley, the sound of a male voice choir floated over the garden. "I've got the Red Army

Choir performing in there," he explained in a tone of apology, waving towards the open door of a large wooden cabin. "I'll ask them to pipe down, politely." And he hurried into the shed and turned the music off.

Dooberry got out a camera and a notebook, took a couple of photos and scribbled some notes. It was an ambitious structure, not your usual self-build job: double-fronted, two large windows, pitched roof with gable end overhanging a verandah. But although it filled the bottom end of the garden, he could tell at once without needing to measure that it was within the permitted dimensions for temporary structures.

The question was what was going on inside.

"It's a shed and a half, isn't it?" said Phelan appearing in the door. "Come on in and have a look around."

This was not the sort of reception Dooberry was used to and it made him uncomfortable. He could feel his mask of professional composure slipping.

The complainant had mentioned large canvases, and there was a stack of them leaning up against the wall opposite the entrance with the top one facing outwards.

Dooberry squinted at it. The picture was a swirling mass of light and colour, but he had absolutely no idea what it was of. Were those sheets hanging on a line or ghostly apparitions? Whatever they were, they were not a business proposition. Who in their right mind would pay money for that?

There was a smaller canvas on the easel that looked equally messy, but what caught Dooberry's attention were two little pictures propped on a shelf above the big canvas to the right of the door. One was of a street of coloured houses leading uphill, the other of a river with bridges that looked like Paris.

With both of them, you could tell what they were – and even to Dooberry's untutored eye, their styles were different. The two paintings were obviously by different people and, when he went over to look, the signatures said so.

The Paris one was legible: it said 'Marquet'. The other

one with the hill he couldn't decipher. It looked a bit like 'Flamingo' without the 'o'.

"These yours?" he asked.

The man looked sheepish.

"They're copies. Copies of paintings by famous artists I've been asked to make for a collector who can't afford the real thing. When he painted this picture," he pointed at the houses, "Maurice de Vlaminck couldn't give 'em away, now they go for tens of millions."

So that was his name. Dooberry had never heard of him. But then he'd never heard of half the artists whose pictures were said to be worth millions in the papers when they were stolen from galleries.

A suspicion was forming in his mind.

"We've had reports of people coming and going."

Phelan raised both arms and gestured around the shed like a conjuror, as if to prove it was empty.

"Quiet as the grave. I'm a solitary soul."

He was lying.

The neighbour had reported seeing gangs of people carrying pictures out of the place and receiving payment. Dooberry had stumbled on something bigger than a planning issue. This was a matter for the police.

Chapter XXXV

Daniel knew there was something wrong from the light, or the absence of it.

Light usually came into the hallway through the living room windows, but although the door to the living room stood open the hallway was dark. There were no blinds on the windows, since Daniel had never got round to buying any. What was blocking the light was a piece of hardboard with a note from his landlord reading: 'BREAK IN Wednesday evening. Police informed.'

Glass littered the desk where his laptop had been. He usually hid it when he went out, but he'd only popped to the shops.

Daniel felt faint. He hobbled over to the sofa, picking his way on crutches through the papers strewn across the floor. His desk drawers were gaping open and the carpet around them was awash with pictures of sheds.

The thesis was backed up, thank God, but everything else – three years of his life – was gone, apart from what was in his phone.

It buzzed.

'Just checking you got home OK. x Yasmin'

'Sort of OK, thanks. Flat broken into, computer gone.'

It rang.

"Don't touch anything, I'm coming over to look before the

local constabulary get their big fat fingers into everything. What's the address?"

Daniel told her.

"Be with you in 20."

Before he could reply she'd rung off.

Wha-a-a-at?

Yasmin was coming to his flat.

The feeling of faintness gave way to a wave of panic. On a normal day the place looked like it had been burgled. How much of this squalor could be attributed to thieves?

There was nothing for it but to disobey police instructions. He scuttled about on his crutches sweeping up dirty socks and boxers, stuffing them into gaps behind the books in the bookcase, then shoving mouldy coffee mugs and half-empty beer cans under the sofa.

This was no way to welcome the woman you loved.

He got out the hoover and looked at it.

Left hand, right crutch? Right hand, left crutch?

Left hand, right crutch seemed the better option until he tried pushing the suction head over the carpet and it stuck in the pile. He experimented with using the vacuum wand as a replacement crutch and dragging his leg in plaster after him. Quasimodo on Quaaludes would have been nimbler.

He threw the hoover back into the cupboard and limped to the bedroom.

When did he last take the sheets to the launderette?

He sniffed the duvet.

One month? Two?

He opened the window.

Now for the kitchen, with a minute to go.

Too late! The doorbell. He threw the dirty pans and dishes into the swing bin and went to get it.

"Hiyah," said Yasmin.

She was dressed in jeans and a maroon leather jacket. She looked beautiful.

"Sami's sleeping over at a friend's house, which is lucky

otherwise I couldn't have come. Crutches!" She looked him up and down. "They rather suit you."

"Thanks."

He moved them back a little reluctantly to let her past.

She started with the area around his desk.

"Your computer's gone, you say. Anything else?"

"Nothing I've noticed. There's nothing else worth stealing."

"The thieves wouldn't know that until they looked. Opportunist thieves do a place over, open all the drawers and cupboards…"

"They might have been disturbed," Daniel interposed, praying she wouldn't start opening the drawers and cupboards.

"Odd," she inspected the broken glass around the window, "it doesn't look like your average break-in. I had a look from the outside and it's a clean break. Done with a glasscutter. A surprisingly professional job for such slim pickings – no disrespect intended," she turned and grinned at Daniel. "My hunch is that they won't have left prints."

The doorbell rang.

"Sounds as if we're about to find out," she called from the hallway as she went to get it.

"Good evening – DC Desai, Art & Antiques Squad," she introduced herself to two police officers standing outside. "The victim is a friend of mine."

"Been in the wars, I see," said the older officer to Daniel.

"Yes, that as well. Not my lucky week."

"Cup of tea?" asked Yasmin.

She had taken over.

While the senior officer interviewed him and the junior one dusted for prints, Daniel could hear her moving around the bedroom and kitchen. He didn't know if this was how it felt to be violated, but it certainly felt worse than being burgled.

When the dusting was over, she returned with four mugs of tea and a crumpled bag with a spoonful of sugar in the bottom.

"No milk," she apologized. "There was a carton but I decided against it, unless anyone fancies cottage cheese in their tea."

She wrinkled her nose at Daniel.

"Found anything?"

"Not a sausage skin," said the senior officer, "they were wearing gloves. A cut above your average N4 thief – round here they're mostly either kids or crackheads. How new was the computer?"

"Three years old."

"Not worth anything then."

"Except to me."

"Or someone who wanted the information on it," put in Yasmin.

The senior officer smirked at the junior one. Detectives saw master criminals everywhere.

"What information was on it?" he asked Daniel with an air of condescension.

"My thesis."

The junior officer was picking photographs off the floor and looking at them. The senior officer cast a disinterested eye over his shoulder.

"And what was that on?"

"Sheddism."

He hoped they wouldn't want an explanation, but they waited.

"Sheds in the history of art."

"Blimey! They'll be doing thesises on garden fencing next. You won't need to go to uni to do it, you can just B&Q it."

He addressed the last remark with a smirk to his junior colleague, who was tidying the photos onto the desk.

Daniel tried a smile. Yasmin's face told him not to bother.

"Contents insurance?"

"Err, no," said Daniel.

"Bad luck, mate. Still, you never know, it might show up. If something's not worth selling it often gets dumped in the nearest bin. Might be worth asking your neighbours before the bin men come."

Daniel nodded.

"If we find out anything more we'll let you know. If it's the usual gang of hoodlums they're all underage. Nothing we can do about them, and they know it."

"Thanks anyway," said Daniel.

Yasmin saw them out, then went on with the tidying of the photos while Daniel watched her helplessly from the sofa.

"If you're hungry," she said when she'd finished, "I'll cook you supper."

"What with?" he heard himself asking.

It sounded rude, but it was genuine surprise. Last time he looked in the fridge there was a can of beer and a radish.

A small frown of impatience knitted Yasmin's eyebrows.

"There are *shops*! I passed one on the corner. We can talk about this," she waved at the window, "over dinner."

Before he could answer she had let herself out.

Daniel hardly had time to transfer his dirty laundry from the bookcase in the living room to the laundry bin in the bedroom and to shake out the duvet before she was back, weighed down by two bulging carrier bags.

"How did you get in?"

"I left the door open. No point in shutting it after the horse has bolted."

"What have you got in there?" he gawped at the bags. "You've bought the whole shop!"

"In your present state, you qualify for home help," she pushed past him with the bags, "and for a single mum this counts as a fun night out."

He followed her meekly into the kitchen, where she heaved the bags onto the counter and itemised the contents as she unpacked.

"Milk. Butter. Eggs. Bacon. Bread. Apples. Mushrooms. Potatoes. Lettuce. Tomatoes. Toilet rolls," she looked up at him, "I think of everything. And a bottle of Spar's best Pinot Grigio. Tonight's menu, in case you're wondering, is mushroom omelette with boiled potatoes and salad, followed by…" she reached into the bottom of the last bag and pulled out a carton "…Häagen-Dazs pralines and cream ice cream. I hope you don't have a nut allergy. They had cookies and cream but this is nicer."

"You're amazing."

Daniel watched speechless with admiration as she prized open the frosted-up freezer compartment and rammed in the ice cream carton, then pulled open the fridge, picked a wrinkled radish off the top shelf, squinted at it, held it up for his inspection and without waiting for a verdict, flipped the swing bin lid and tossed it in. She replaced it on the empty shelf with the Pinot Grigio.

"There," she said in a tone of semi-finality, and began opening and shutting kitchen cupboards. "Where do you keep your pans?"

Daniel sat down, propped his crutches on the counter and pointed mutely at the bin.

She pulled off the lid and fished out a pot and a frying pan, followed by a spatula, a wooden spoon and a stack of dishes. She transferred them to the sink, squeezed on Fairy Liquid and turned on the tap.

"If you'd kept your computer in the bin, it wouldn't have been stolen."

Dinner tasted like a feast to Daniel; the queasiness he had felt all evening vanished. While they ate she asked him about the accident and the burglary. She seemed to think it was more than a run of bad luck.

"What was on the computer?"

"Three years of work on the thesis, including pictures, all backed up, thank God. Research on articles for *Marquette*. And all my personal data, contacts, photographs."

Yasmin looked worried.

"I suppose you know about Orlovsky's links to the Russian mafia? Five years ago the Serious Fraud Office tried to pin a charge of money laundering on him but the case never came to court: the key witnesses all lost their memories except for one, who lost his life when his business burned down. I tried to warn you, but you wouldn't listen. I never thought you'd get yourself in this deep."

"Aren't you being a little bit alarmist?" protested Daniel, secretly enjoying her concern. "I'm an intern on a two-bit art magazine with a readership, in a good month, of under 5,000. I'm not a threat to the Russian mafia. I'm a nobody."

"You'd be better protected if you were somebody. Do you know the average length of the police response time on an 'I'-grade 'immediate response' 999 call? Twelve minutes. Longer than it would take you to get out of the house and halfway down the street, even in your present condition. Assuming you were given the chance to get out.

"I think I'll stay the night, if it's OK with you."

This was not how it was meant to happen.

"I can sleep on the couch," offered Daniel.

"With that leg," she laughed, "you wouldn't fit on it. You'll be better off sleeping in the bed with me. If there's any breaking and entering it'll be through the front and we'll have time to get out through the bedroom window. If we shut it after us, they'll think the place is empty. Just remember to take your crutches with you. What does your bedroom back onto?"

"The East Coast Main Line."

"Perfect. If they stake out the place we've got an escape route."

Daniel didn't argue, he was lost for words. This was not how it was meant to happen, but it was fine by him.

Better than fine, it was utter magic.

Amazing what can be done with a leg in plaster. Afterwards they drifted off to sleep like babies, until a sudden loud crash by the bedroom door had them both sitting bolt upright in bed.

Yasmin was out of bed and across the room before Daniel could disentangle his leg from the duvet.

She was back in bed almost as quickly. The rumble of a passing freight train had dislodged Daniel's crutches from the radiator where he had propped them for the night.

When he woke the following morning, she was gone. In the kitchen he found a note on the dirty dishes:

"DO NOT THROW AWAY. Can be reused after washing."

Chapter XXXVI

'MYSTERY DEEPENS OVER 'WISE BEQUEST' TO STATE – BERNARD ORLOVSKY REVEALED AS DONOR'.

The Telegraph had picked up the *Marquette* story, as had all the other papers arranged on Nigel Vouvray-Jones's desk in readiness for his arrival that Tuesday morning. 'MONKEY BUSINESS OVER WISE LEGACY,' insinuated *The Guardian* over a picture of a stuffed monkey with its fingers in its ears, a work by contemporary taxidermist Poppy Vaughan titled 'Hear No Evil'. 'WISE BUYS BY BERNARD ORLOVSKY?' questioned *The Independent* under a photo of the dealer getting into his car.

The other papers just recycled Daniel Colvin's article, but *The Times* correspondent, under the headline 'FROM RUSSIA WITH LOVE', had done some research of her own and drawn attention to an exhibition of Russian contemporary art being planned for the State Gallery's new extension the following autumn. Reports had been confirmed by sources in Moscow but not by the State. "It's some way off," the State spokesperson had said, "and the programme has yet to be finalised."

The media furore was a small source of satisfaction in what, for Vouvray-Jones, had been a wretched week. Anything that made Jeremy Gaunt feel bad right now made Vouvray-Jones feel better. He blamed the State director for what he saw as the hopeless mismanagement of the Boegemann exhibition the previous summer. If there was an opposite to a buzz, he'd succeeded in creating it.

True, the timing of Wise's death had been disastrous and the fact that it had dominated the arts pages that week could not be blamed on the State. But the Boegemann show had been badly curated, badly presented and hopelessly publicised. It had left the critics cold and the arts correspondents – who could usually rely on Boegemann for a salacious story – in the lurch.

God alone knew what had got into the Dutchman, but he had conducted himself impeccably throughout. The combined result was that last week's RDV auction had been a washout. Two smaller pictures – uncharacteristic flower paintings with red touches – sold for above estimate. Only a handful of other lots reached their reserves, leaving the auction house holding an aborted baby, a bunch of hand-grenades and yards and yards of concrete barriers and razor wire.

Was it any wonder, in the present climate, that collectors craved colour and preferred Matisse's comfortable armchair to an electric one, unless it was nicely tinted by Andy Warhol? Thank heaven for Derain, the colour of money. Everything was riding on that now. Duval had really taken it to the wire, hanging onto the picture for so long. The auction house had been left with just two weeks to fly the painting between interested collectors in Switzerland, Japan and Qatar.

Still, with luck the wait would have sharpened their appetites as it had sharpened his. He anticipated the painting's arrival with relish. Crispin Finch had been sniffing around, pestering him for a look. He was hoping to splash the story in November's *Marquette*, and now that *Marquette* was hot the mainstream press might follow. The history of the picture's reappearance made such great copy that even Cassandra Pemberton hadn't fucked it up.

In the photographs Duval had had taken for the catalogue the picture appeared in pristine condition. It didn't look as if it had sustained much damage, but James was a stickler for conservation and had insisted on overseeing the work himself. He was still fussing over the Modigliani nude Nigel had hoped to include in the same auction.

A disappointment, but one mustn't be greedy. That treat would have to wait for next February's sale, for which he had three other plums lined up: a Vlaminck *Hillside with Houses*, a Marquet *Pont Neuf in the Snow* and a Jawlensky *Still Life with Fruit and Flowers*. Cassandra Pea-brain Pemberton was working on the catalogue entries now. She could write what she liked; the works spoke for themselves. He'd seen a scan of the Jawlensky on Friday – it was a cracker.

No doubt about it, James had rescued him from the brink of disaster. He owed him lunch.

Chapter XXXVII

"It's great you're in the police force, Mum. All my mates except for Kieran are going to boring shops and offices and I'm going out catching thieves."

It was Take Your Child to Work Day and Yasmin and Sami were in the car on their way to Bounds Green to investigate a suspect. A Haringey Council officer following up a planning complaint had reported seeing what he thought were two stolen paintings in a large garden shed behind a house off Bounds Green Road. The paintings were signed 'Marquet' and 'Flamingk' – famous artists, apparently, with pictures in museums – and the householder, a Mr Patrick Phelan, had been acting suspiciously.

Under normal circumstances Yasmin would never have dreamed of taking Sami to a possible crime scene, but from the account of the planning officer, a Mr Hank Dooberry, the owner of the shed was a crazy old artist. With crazy old artists Yasmin instinctively felt on safe ground. And there was no one to leave Sami with at the office.

Anyway he was a smart kid. He could look out for himself.

"Mind what you say when we get there," Yasmin eyed him in the rearview window of the Nissan Micra as they drove north up the Blackhorse Road. "Remember I'm your mum, not a policewoman – we're going to enquire about art classes. Keep your eyes peeled but try not to look suspicious."

Sami widened his eyes into a semblance of innocence.

"That's good!" laughed Yasmin, "except it makes me suspect *you*. The point is, we don't know the suspect has done anything. The law says you're innocent until proven guilty."

"The law for grown-ups," said Sami.

* * * * * * * * * *

No.15 The Mall was a small semi-detached late Victorian red brick villa, set back from the road behind a screen of trees. Dooberry had said the shed was accessible from the side alley and sure enough, when they went round the side they found a sign saying 'THE SHED' in splodgy writing and a chain saying 'PULL'.

Sami pulled, and giggled at the clang of cowbells. This was going to be more fun than Azeem's day with his mum in Iceland, though not as much fun as Kieran's with his Dad at Kwik Fit.

* * * * * * * * * *

Like the sanctuary bell at the elevation of the host, the ringing of the cowbell coincided with the final brushstroke that put the seal, as it were, on The Seventh Seal. Pat's release from copying duty had opened the floodgates, sweeping away the psychological obstacles of a lifetime with the force of the resulting surge. He had never experienced a rush of inspiration like it – the roar was audible. Six of the Seals had now gone to glory and only the Fourth – The Pale Horse – was still kicking against the pricks. But its days of resistance were numbered and it knew it. The momentum from now on was on Pat's side.

Ten o'clock on a Thursday morning. Who could it be?

Things had gone quiet since the planning inspector's visit but Pat had a feeling he wasn't out of the woods. Dino had told him that if a shed breached planning regulations the council had the authority to take it down. If they demolished

The Shed of Revelation at this crucial juncture The Pale Horse might never pass the finishing post. Pat hadn't liked the way the inspector had looked at the Vlaminck, even though it was no business of his. Who could object to an 8x10in scrap of canvas? It wasn't in anyone's way, not even Ron's. Still, he was sure his neighbour was behind it. Crabby old bugger should get himself a woman, find a better place to poke his nose than into other people's affairs.

The bell clanged again, insistently, and for a moment as he crossed the lawn the idea popped into Pat's head that it might be the police. So it was with relief that he saw, framed in the fox flap, a pair of red ballerina pumps and a pair of child's trainers.

The relief turned to pleasure when he pulled back the door to reveal a dusky green-eyed odalisque and a wide-eyed boy. He stood back to frame the vision in the doorway against the late September light of the tree-lined street.

Venus and Cupid. A touch more vegetation, a few fewer clothes – a gold choker for her, a bow and wings for him – and there you had it, Cranach was your uncle.

"I've heard about your art class," said Venus, "and I'm interested in joining."

"Mum's an artist," explained Cupid.

"Yes, but *I'd like to be a better one*," Venus added, glaring at Cupid.

"We'd all like that," said Pat, letting out a sigh.

"When are your classes?"

"Friday mornings 10.00 to 1.00."

"Mum's at work then," put in Cupid. Venus trod on his foot.

Clumsy, thought Pat, for someone with such dainty tootsies.

"I could take time off... or perhaps you do one-to-one tuition?"

That was more like it! Imagine this beauty dropping into his lap. He wondered if she'd exchange free tuition for modelling. He pictured her with a camellia behind her ear – no, on second

159

thoughts a marigold, Herb of the Sun, to complement the sea-green of her eyes.

"I haven't introduced myself," she held out her hand. "Yasmin Desai. This is my son Sami."

A marigold behind the ear, and a wreath of jasmine. Pat took the hand in both of his and squeezed.

"Why don't you come in? I was just making a cup of tea. You can look around and see what you'd be signing up to."

"That would be great, if we're not disturbing you."

Pat led the way down the alley towards The Shed.

"This is the operational hub and the seat of inspiration: The Shed of Revelation. Go on in and I'll bring the tea. Mind the wet paint," he said to Sami. "Sugar?"

Sami nodded. "For me, not Mum."

"Right you are," said Pat. Of course Cupid took sugar.

He saluted and disappeared into the house.

* * * * * * * * *

Yasmin stood on the lawn in front of the shed. It was certainly imposing. Not easy to achieve in creosoted clapboard, but this suburban structure somehow pulled it off. There was something about the proportions. Were they Palladian? She took some photos for Daniel from different angles.

"He's a funny man," whispered Sami as they climbed the steps to the verandah. "Did you see his hair? And he's wearing purple socks."

"He's an artist," said Yasmin, opening the shed door and finding herself face to face with the evidence. A canvas leant against the wall opposite the entrance, gleaming with juicy freshly applied paint. Yasmin had never seen anything quite like it. The elongated format and visionary colour reminded her of the decorative panels of Odilon Redon, but this was Redon with a bomb under him. Instead of Redon's dreamy verticals this picture was all diagonals, threatening to tear the composition apart with the tension of opposing forces.

At the top, a massive angel's head thrust out of purple shadow with fiery locks streaming upwards in a conflagration of orange and yellow. To the right of the head, a river of blue and red snaked around the form of a flaming mountain into a deep black pit on the bottom left. From out of the pit a giant blue hand reached up, releasing an inky swarm of insect-like creatures that merged with the smoke from the burning mountain. On the bottom right a herd of wild green horses, also aflame, charged past the pit behind a fluttering red pennant. In the eye of this compositional storm, at the picture's centre, the angel's hand gripped a golden scroll, while beneath the scroll its two muscular feet were firmly planted, one on the earth, the other in the water. In the picture's top left hand corner, on a counter-diagonal, a bunch of golden trumpets blared in the angel's ear, while on the top right was a single point of stillness: a triangle of translucent green worn like an ornament in the angel's hair.

It was a prodigious vision, seething with life. It knocked the breath out of Yasmin; it even silenced Sami.

"This is amazing," gasped Yasmin when Phelan returned with the tea.

"Do you think so?"

For someone whose imagination had stirred up this maelstrom he sounded strangely shy and hesitant.

"It's awesome," said Sami, studying the cloud of inky creatures and trying to decide if they were locusts or scorpions. He'd dissected a locust at school.

Phelan looked delighted, but a little shaken.

"You're the first to see it," he said. "I've just finished it. It's The Seventh Seal."

He made it sound like it had fallen out of his sleeve and standing looking at it now, he could almost believe it.

"Is this what you teach in your classes?"

For a moment Yasmin had forgotten what she came for and was wondering if there was some way she could join the class.

"I try to," he handed out the tea mugs, "though I can't say I've always learned the lessons myself."

"Can we see the others?" Yasmin pointed to the canvases behind.

"The ones that are finished," he replied rather coyly. "We're not officially ready for the grand unveiling."

He put down his tea.

"You're witnessing a historic moment," he confided to Sami, "the culmination of a lifetime's work." And with a flourish like a conjuror revealing the outcome of a card trick, he spread seven canvases out with their faces to the wall and twiddled them around, the fourth excepted, one by one. At every twiddle the harmony of hues grew richer as new chromatic notes were added to the scale. Where the fourth canvas stood there was an audible silence, like the striking of a dead key on a piano.

Yasmin had thought of herself as a colourist, by English standards, but she had never seen colours like this. They seemed to pulsate and hover on a cushion of air a centimetre above the picture surface.

"Your colours are magical," she said, "they're alive. How do you do it?"

"You listen to them," he answered. "Sometimes they squabble and need separating, like children. Sometimes they get along fine, start a productive conversation and sometimes, if you're very lucky, they sing."

Sami stifled a laugh, then stared and gulped. The figure of a topless woman was peeking out from behind the canvas turned to the wall. He blushed and prodded Yasmin, who followed his gaze. There on the floor, in a gap between The Fourth and The Fifth Seals, a Modigliani nude was reclining. The top half of a Modigliani nude, to be precise. The bottom half was blank except for a black and white photo attached to the stretcher with masking tape.

It brought Yasmin back to reality with a bang.

"Do you mind if I take a picture?" she asked, pulling out her phone.

"Be my guest," said Phelan, crossing his legs and resting one elbow languidly along the top of The First Seal like an English milord posing for a portrait by Pompeo Batoni. In that position, Sami noticed that his purple socks had started a squabble with the scarlet cape of the First Horseman of the Apocalypse.

* * * * * * * * * *

"I think he's innocent," said Sami in the car on the way home. "He doesn't look like a thief to me. He's a bit weird, though," he giggled, "he says colours can talk."

"He may not be innocent," said Yasmin, "but you're right, he's not a thief."

Patrick Phelan was no thief. He was a faker and, from the look of that Modigliani, an extremely good one. She'd been asleep on the job; if it hadn't been for Sami she'd have missed it. She was so blown away by his paintings she forgot what she came for.

"I owe you, Sami. Take Your Child to Work Day is supposed to be for teaching kids about their parents' jobs, but you taught me something about mine today. I'd have missed that picture of the naked lady if it wasn't for you. Noticing stuff like that is what makes a good detective, and your mum took her eye off the ball. This is worth a pack of cola bottles."

"Something else I've noticed, Mum," said Sami later as they turned into Ilfracombe Road. "There's a white van behind us and the same van was following us on the way there."

Yasmin turned just in time to see the back of a white tranny disappearing into the road bordering the park, too late to catch the number-plate. But she thought she saw a patch of fresh white paint on the side, as if a logo had been painted over.

"Are you sure it was the same van?" she asked Sami uneasily. "There are a lot of white transit vans on the road."

"Yes, but they don't all have the same number-plate."

Take Your Child to Work Day, Lesson 2. Yasmin got a pencil and a petrol receipt out of the glove compartment and handed them to Sami, who wrote down a number and handed them back.

"A packs of cola bottles, and some yellow belly snakes."

Chapter XXXVIII

It happened so quickly Sami didn't know what hit him. One minute he was dribbling his precious football down the road trying to break his personal speed-dribble record of 15 seconds from the front door to the park, the next he had a blanket over his head and was being bundled into the back of a van. By some primal reflex he managed to grab the football, but his school bag with his mobile phone was left on the porch. He had no way of contacting Mrs Dudek downstairs, who looked after him on schooldays until his mum got back from work.

Sami felt the van swing left and left and right and left, and as it hurled him one way, then the other he tried to keep a mental map of where he was going. He got as far as the Blackhorse Road, then his GPS lost contact.

At that point he started to worry about what to do.

He'd heard of kidnapping. It happened to rich kids, mostly, the children of celebrities, and from what he'd heard they were usually tied up. But Sami wasn't, and it set him thinking. What he was thinking was that when they got to wherever they were going, the van doors would have to be opened to get him out. That, he realised, would be his make-or-break moment. He'd know it was coming because the van would slow and stop, he'd hear the engine being turned off and the men – he thought there were two of them – getting out.

He worked out a plan. It involved a sacrifice but in his present situation he had no option.

Unfortunately Sami's plan had a flaw. What he hadn't anticipated was that when the van slowed and stopped, the doors would be opened inside a docking bay. Not being familiar with the sound of garage roller-shutter doors – the family Micra was parked on the street – he had no time to develop a Plan B. So he stayed poised to put Plan A into operation with the football tucked under his right foot.

No sooner were the van doors opened than Sami's precious football came flying under the full force of his boot smack into the face of a burly man in a beanie hat. Before the man could work out what had hit him Sami had jumped down from the tail flap and ducked away, to find his escape route blocked by a roller-shutter door.

By now the driver had got out and made a lunge for Sami, but a feint from the kid caused him to slip and drop his keys. Sami swiped them, found the attached remote control keypad, waved it towards the door and jabbed at the buttons. To his amazement the roller mechanism clanked into motion and as the door lifted off the ground he slithered under. Through the gap he could see the football rolling towards him. He willed it closer, but just as it inched within his grasp the driver got up and made a dash for the door.

Sami bid goodbye to his beloved football and jabbed the remote. He heard the clanking of the roller door behind him and didn't hang around for long enough to see it clank shut on the driver's foot.

* * * * * * * * * *

When Yasmin got home she found him sitting on the sofa in his Gunners baseball cap, looking gutted.

"I've lost the Arsenal ball," he moped, "the one Mr Burningham gave me."

His mother didn't seem remotely interested.

"Mrs Dudek rang me. Where have you been? What happened?"
She sounded breathless and upset.
"You've torn your jacket. Have you been in a fight?"
"Sort of."
"Oh Sami! Tell Mum what happened."
She flopped onto the sofa beside him, and the story came out.
"So how did you get back home?" she asked, astonished.
"I ran until I got to an Underground station and squeezed through the barrier behind a lady with one of those wheelie case things. When I got to our end I said I'd lost my mum as I was playing Fruit Ninja when you got off."
"What station was it?"
"Walthamstow."
"No, I mean the one you got on at."
"The Arsenal station."
He meant the Angel.
"Did you notice the name of the street the garage was in?"
"No Mum, I was too busy running. Oh, but here," he reached in his jacket, "I got the keys."
He dropped them on the couch.
"They fell out of this bloke's pocket when I tripped him up. I couldn't see his face – it was dark in there and he was wearing a Beanie hat. People in Beanie hats all look the same. Like idiots."
He squeezed the peak of his baseball cap and pulled it down over his eyes.
Yasmin's fear and shock dissolved in admiration.
"Well, I never… Sami the adventure hero!"
She opened her arms for a hug, which the hero accepted.
"Oh, and I left my schoolbag on the porch," he added.
"I brought it in," she said, pointing to the passage where it was hanging on its usual peg. She picked the keys off the sofa with a tissue and bagged them for the lab. "Anyway you won't be needing it for a while. No school tomorrow, you're off to your Nan's in Leicester."
She picked up the phone and dialled her mum.

Chapter XXXIX

Pat whistled as he crossed the leaf-strewn lawn with the bundle of newspapers under his arm. He never read the papers – he found them an unnecessary distraction – but Grant passed on his old ones for studio use.

Now that the Seals were into the final straight, Pat was fired up with a new idea for a series of paintings of nudes in allotments. A series of paintings had a certain gravitas. Think of Monet: it was only when he started painting in series that people began to take him 'seriesly'. Pat grinned; he'd try that one out on Wolf on Friday. It was about his level.

Criminal waste, he thought, as he passed the pear tree hanging its autumn boughs heavy with fruit over the hedge from his neighbour's garden. Those few branches were the sole survivors of Ron's relentless campaign against rampant vegetation. Ron had a pathological fear of rampancy. He had pruned all the branches on his side back to stumps so that the tree now leant lopsidedly into Pat's garden, trailing its tresses of reddening fruit like a Titian-haired temptress leaning over to brush her hair.

On this fine autumn day the scene cried out for the Renoir woodland nymph-in-the-nip treatment. What Pat wouldn't give to stretch Irene beneath it and let the Indian summer light dapple her thighs! An impossible dream on a Saturday morning, when his neighbour would be on the blower to the porn squad before the tip of the brush had kissed the canvas.

Pat was musing on Marvell's *Thoughts in a Garden* as he climbed the sun-warmed steps to the verandah. Since that day with Maisie in the allotment those fruity verses had been ripening at the back of his brain, diffusing an aroma of *déjeuner sur l'herbe*.

"What wondrous life is this I lead!" he declaimed out loud when the door of The Shed was safely shut behind him. "Ripe apples drop about my head; the luscious clusters of the vine upon my mouth do crush their wine."

A marvel, that Marvell. A sexy beast, a prince among poets and MP for Hull into the bargain. Those were the days! He wondered idly what sort of poetry the Right Honourable Member for Hull would be writing now.

The three allotment sketches he had made with Maisie were propped on the plan chest to the left of his easel, on which a prepared canvas was already resting with the greenery blocked in around an unpainted triangle reserved for Irene.

She was due at 10.

"Meanwhile the mind from pleasure less withdraws into its happiness," he intoned over the accompaniment of crumpling newsprint as he tore the old paper off his painting table to replace it with new. A fresh start always gave Pat the virtuous feeling of a housewife tucking in crisply laundered sheets. This was the good bit, the new beginning, when ideas careered freely through the brain before reality slammed on the brakes.

He picked a paper off the top of the pile, opened it out and flattened it on the table surface, then went to organise his palette. Squeezing out glistening heaps of paint was a physical pleasure akin, he imagined, to the satisfaction a baby must feel, on rising from the potty, to discover he's deposited a perfect turd. A fresh-laid palette was like a smorgasbord for a psychedelic dung beetle.

Burnt Umber, Burnt Sienna, Yellow Ochre, Naples Yellow, Zinc White (warmer than cold unfeeling Titanium), Terre Verte, Viridian, Cinnabar Green (the colour of sunlight through sappy spring leaves), Cobalt Blue, Ultramarine, Cobalt Violet (the colour of love all year round), Alizarin, Magenta, Indian Red, Cadmium Red, Cadmium Orange… The names on the paint tubes resonated with a poetry as ancient as the thousand names of Vishnu.

Irene floated in on the dot of 10, punctual as the tide. While she undressed behind the screen, Pat studied his sketches for elements to complete the composition.

The viewpoint was inside the potting shed: sylvan nymph glimpsed through open door luxuriating under a canopy of apples, with receding rows of bean canes lending depth on the right and an autumn cabbage patch, with that milky bloom, returning the eye caressingly to the foreground. The triangle formed by the nude on the sun-streaked grass was to be contained within a larger triangle extending from the shed door towards the vanishing point of the bean cane and cabbage rows outside the frame, leading the eye and the imagination towards a fertile field of boundless possibilities.

Leaving the pub with Dino the week before, Pat had spotted a roll of old Astroturf from the so-called beer garden lying out on the street for the rubbish men. What a piece of serendipity! A perfect nymph carpet. He'd carried it home and hosed it down in the garden until it came up sparkling, good as new. Its greenness put the grass on the lawn to shame. Halfway through the op, of course, Ron came out and poked his nose through the gap in the hedge.

"Spring-cleaning the lawn for autumn," was Pat's explanation. "Look, no weeds!"

The nose withdrew without a word while the rest of Ron's mug composed itself into a silent harrumph.

Miserable bastard. No one could say Pat didn't work at neighbourly relations. He tried.

When Irene came padding out in her old silk kimono, the greensward was spread out on the floor to welcome her.

"See, old cat, I've got a carpet for your bower."

"It's a bit prickly," said Irene as she lay down.

"We'll soon fix that," said Pat and nipped over to the house for his green bathmat.

He arranged it under her elbows and hips and stood back to admire the effect.

"La Luxe!"

By God Irene was a good model. She looked as relaxed as if she was lying in clover.

"You're a star."

He kissed her on the top of the head and crossed to the easel with spring in his step and a song in his heart.

There is something in the way the human head sits on the neck and the neck on the shoulders that tells you most of what you need to know about a person. Those two conjunctions, when correctly aligned, make up two-thirds of the sum of human beauty, and by that measure Irene was Venus herself. As soon as Pat had positioned her reclining figure in the triangular space reserved under the apple, those were the points – the cruxes of the matter – on which he got to work.

He imagined late summer light slanting through leafy branches, dappling the shoulders and breasts, underpainted in green, with pink and yellow, while the neck was cast into warm shadow – burnt sienna, Indian red and violet – by the head. Touches of magenta and cadmium orange on the shoulders; flecks of Naples yellow brushing the left breast, where the sun struck through, and the tip of the chin. Wavelets of cinnabar green dancing under the chin where sun mingled with shade, the secret meeting place of chiaro and scuro – a place of assignation, cool and mossy.

As he got into the rhythm of the broken colour and the hues began to weave their chromatic spell, Pat drank deep of a familiar intoxication. When it came on in a rush like this there was nothing else like it, except sex in sunlight. It should be bottled. He was beginning to feel quite pleasantly tipsy when, reaching over to clean his brush on the newspaper, he experienced a sensation like being really drunk.

He was seeing double.

Looking up at him from the table was the very same head on the very same shoulders he had just been painting, under the headline: 'RARE DEGAS SELLS TO KHALEEJ MUSEUM FOR $40m'.

Pat stared at the paper, stone cold sober. The spell was shattered.

"Are you alright, love?" asked Irene.

"Fine," he said faintly.

"You sound a bit funny."

"You know me, funny as they come."

The attempt at a joke stuck in his throat like phlegm. Whatever happened Irene mustn't see this.

"Lousy juggler, spilt the sodding turps." He cleared the painting gear off the table, lifted off the top sheet of newspaper and dropped it into the gap behind the Seals to look at later.

The sun had set on Pat's allotment. He went through the motions, but the magic hour had passed. The colours turned to sludge on his brush. Even Irene had caught the mood and stiffened. The life went out of her luxuriant flesh; it sagged.

So that was Marty's game. How hadn't he seen it? It wasn't as if he didn't have enough experience. But this was on a different scale even for Marty. Well they were in it together now, up to their necks, unless Pat shopped him. And how could you shop your own flesh and blood?

It was all his fault, he'd been a rotten father. He should have put a stop to it years ago, but he let the boy run wild and now it was 30 years too late. He'd got him out of scrapes in the past, done a brilliant line in letters to the Head and charmed the pants (literally in one instance) off his form teachers. But letters and pant-charming wouldn't get them out of this one.

This was a crime of a more serious order.

At lunchtime he sent Irene home saying he wasn't feeling well; he must have overindulged the night before. And it was true that he felt sick to the pit of his stomach. It wasn't so much the realization that he'd been used by his own son as the confirmation that someone would pay $40m for a Phelan Degas, when they wouldn't pay $400 for a Phelan Phelan.

Chapter XXXX

The pale October sun filtered through the broken Venetian blind into the bedroom, warming the rumpled duvet and striking the empty interior of the open wardrobe. On its path across the carpet the shaft of light illuminated a trail of socks and boxers spilling out of an open chest of drawers, on top of which, in shadow, stood a half-drunk mug of coffee and a plate of toast. A late bumblebee vibrated the slats of the blind as it made futile assaults on the closed window.

A smell of sleep hung over the room, which was itself slumbering as rooms will do when vacated by their occupants. Try walking back into one quietly and you'll catch it at it. Vacated rooms resent unanticipated intrusions. And at 9.17 on this Saturday morning, the slumbers of this particular room were rudely interrupted by an angry voice shouting from the telephone on the bedside table.

"I've just got back from a visit to my aged mother in Wales and found Wednesday's paper. I don't believe it. What the hell did you think you were doing? It's under two weeks to the Derain auction. Couldn't you have waited? Now you've probably blown the whole shebang. The mercy is that the picture's gone to Khaleej where, thank God, no one will know the difference. In case you're thinking of cutting me in, which I doubt, I'd like to make clear that I want no part of this. What I do want from you, now, is an assurance that you won't be springing any more surprises. The merest whiff of that and the whole deal's off. Where are you? I've been trying your mobile all morning. Call me."

But Martin Phelan didn't call because, when James Duval's nerve-jangling voicemail shook his bedroom awake, he was in an Emirates Airbus over Turkey en route to Zubarrah, capital of the Emirate of Khaleej, with a dozen dot paintings crated in the hold. He was over Iraq at 11.20 when a husky voice disturbed the peace for a second time pleading: "Where are you, Marty? I've been trying your mobile since yesterday. Are you OK darling? Call me." And by the time the silence was again interrupted once again by the sound of a throat being cleared and a voice saying wearily: "Dad here, call me," he was on a lounger by the palm-fringed pool of the Falconry Hotel, Zubarrah gazing out over a distant view of the floating cranes that were lazily dumping the breakwater for the Emirate's new Pearl Island development: a 4km pearl drop in the ocean designed to accommodate a dozen hotels, a concert hall, cinema complex, shopping mall, championship golf course and Khaleej's new Museum of Modern Art.

Martin drained his beer and dipped a hairy toe in the water. Time for a swim and a snooze before his evening meeting with the Minister of Culture, Arts and Heritage. What a perfect spot: sea, sand and endless sunshine. No leaking roofs, and no extradition treaty.

Chapter XXXXI

Rushes of adrenaline were rare in the offices of Scotland Yard's Art & Antiques Unit. This was the civilised end of the theft and fraud business, where dirty money was handled in white cotton gloves. Investigations proceeded slowly, conserving energies that, as often as not, investigators knew would be wasted.

The long arm of the law was never so stretched as when a rolled up scrap of canvas costing tens of millions was half-inched by a bunch of Eastern European gangsters. By the time the work was recovered, if ever, it had been tossed like a hot potato along a chain of intermediaries so extended that the individuals involved could convincingly claim never to have touched it.

The Yard's involvement was often merely a matter of form, sometimes quite literally a matter of form-filling. It was the nexus of go-betweens, professional and non-professional, legitimate and criminal, that got the job done. The missing painting was spirited back to the rectangle of wall it had vacated and that was the last one heard of it. A few more facts on the Interpol database, a few more entries on the Police National Computer, but few arrests and no convictions. Chasing global art thieves was a non-contact sport.

And now this. An attempted kidnap right on the Met's doorstep, targeting a valued member of the unit's staff, had jolted the squad into a sudden sense of its own importance. Detective Sergeant Jeff Burningham had a soft spot for DC Desai; he even knew the boy, a bright kid. He had given him the autographed football he'd won in June at the Arsenal Foundation charity raffle.

Burningham took it personally, and he did his utmost to ensure that all available forces were thrown behind the investigation. Desai and the young reporter who broke the story about Bernard Orlovsky's anonymous donation – and got his leg broken for his trouble – had both been given 24-hr police protection. The reporter had been warned off the story; they didn't want to risk any further upsets. And the boy was safe for now with his grandmother in Leicester.

The number plates, if the boy had remembered right, were fake but the make of keypad and the lead that the lock-up was in the Islington area had led police to a storage facility beside the canal in Wharf Road, N1. The electronic entry code had been changed, but when officers forcibly entered the premises they found the bodies of two men hanging from a crossbeam. The men, both white males in their 30s, were stripped to their underpants, with no other means of identification than an Umbro beanie hat found on the floor beneath one of the bodies.

Fingerprint tests revealed the Beanie-wearer to be a petty crook going by the name of Andrew Davies, who had been in the Scrubs two years earlier for GBH. He had worked as a club bouncer and a glam wrestler under the stage name Rock Steelman, and had recently been temping as a doorman for upmarket security agency ArtSafe, used by leading London galleries including Orlovsky's.

Since developing into a murder inquiry, the investigation had widened. Interpol had been alerted. Orlovsky was widely believed to have underworld connections, although nothing had ever been pinned on him. For the time being, discretion was the better part of valour. Reports of the two deaths had been kept to a minimum, with coverage so far confined to

The Islington Gazette. If the nationals got whiff of an Orlovsky connection, the investigation could be blown wide open.

There was little to connect the kidnap to Orlovsky, no obvious motive, but then nothing in the art world these days was obvious. The art market's ethics might be those of a car boot sale, but its workings were considerably more complex. At the top end of the market there was no longer such a thing as a simple, transparent, above-board transaction. The repercussions of a single deal could spread out in any number of directions.

In the case of a global operator with multiple irons in the fire, the possible lines of enquiry – and avenues of escape – were endless. Orlovsky wasn't someone you could just slip cuffs on. He wouldn't come quietly; he had powerful friends.

At this point in his career the Detective Sergeant would have liked nothing better than a high-profile arrest at the Orlovsky Gallery with a BBC camera crew in attendance, but if the charge didn't stick the Force would be left with egg on its face. Nothing had ever stuck to Orlovsky. He was as slippery as a jellied conger eel.

Burningham settled in for the long haul.

He made a mental note to get young Desai a new football. A mate of his was on the Arsenal Board.

Chapter XXXXII

On a slow news day, Orlovsky's disappearance made the front pages. 'NO SHOW AT OWN EXHIBITION LAUNCH: art magnate fails to join the dots at Byrne private view' ran the headline in the *Times*. 'SPOT THE MISSING GALLERIST', splashed the *Evening Standard* over a photo of a star-studded gathering floating in a galaxy of coloured dots. 'SPOT OF BOTHER?' queried *The Express*.

The London art world was abuzz with rumours about the mystery absence of the ever-present Orlovsky from the opening of his much-hyped exhibition. Frustratingly for Fay Lacey-Pigott, the only publication not leading on the story was *Marquette*. With unusual courtesy Orlo had staged his vanishing act in good time for the magazine's November deadline. But could she find anyone to cover it? Could she hell.

Daniel, who was still hobbling round the office on crutches, had made an uncharacteristically lame excuse about it being a matter for the police – which, as far as his editor could see, was the whole point. He insisted on finishing the piece he was working on about the meteoric rise of the Khaleeji Royal Family up the ranks of the International Art Movers & Shakers list. As the IAM&S list wasn't published until January, it could have waited.

Daniel's broken leg seemed to have broken his nerve. And Crispin, to Fay's fury, had refused point blank, saying he wouldn't stoop to 'gutter journalism' and persisting with a run-of-the-mill report on the recent sale of the rediscovered Derain for a record £16m marking an upturn in the fortunes of RazzleDeVere.

Gutter journalism! This was what was called news, my dears! The stuff news gatherers were employed to gather. How could a publication boasting the strapline 'First with the Art News' ignore the sudden unexplained disappearance of the leading gallerist who had topped last year's IAM&S list? It would have been pointless to give Bernice the gig, it was beyond her pay grade. So here was the editor at zero hour cobbling together a pitifully under-researched 400 words on what should, by any normal journalistic measure, have been a lead story.

Fay felt like crying. The photograph would have to be blown up. There was an eye-catching shot of 6ft1in model Mawgan Jones attending the launch in a limited edition dot-painted dress specially designed for the occasion by Georgia McClintock. It was better than Orlovsky's ugly mug, and it might pull in a half-page of fashion advertising.

The Derain would have to go on the front page.

Fay called up the image on screen and felt a bit better. It was a beautiful picture.

Chapter XXXXIII

The bookies' odds on Tammy Tinker-Stone to win the Ars Nova had shortened to 11/10. Daniel wondered how the odds were calculated. Bookmakers were not known students of artists' form, although the art and racing worlds had certain things in common. Ruthlessness, corruption, wastage, drugs, losers prematurely put out to grass.

The one artist whose form the bookies were in any position to judge this year was Tinker-Stone, as the other three nominees were all unknown quantities: 'British-based' – the qualification for entry – but variously born in Tunisia, Lithuania and Taiwan.

Tinker-Stone was only the favourite because they'd heard of her, because she was English and had long sleek hair and the sort of good strong teeth that invited a sugar lump. Next most fancied at 13/8 was the Tunisian woman artist A'ishah Madani, nominated for a film about a love affair between a niqab-wearing Muslim and a blinkered horse – an Arab *Equus* set in the Société des Courses Hippiques in Tunis.

The Taiwanese and Lithuanian were rank outsiders at 100-1. But you never knew with the Ars Nova. There had long been mutterings that the race was rigged, the selectors being doped rather than the runners. Not that the selectors needed doping, since they were themselves carefully pre-selected and could be relied upon to be onside.

In the heyday of Cool British Art most of the guests at an event like this would have failed a dope test but, post-recession, austerity was the drug of choice, its endorphin-releasing effects heightened by heart-stopping workout routines in the gym. Austerity didn't stop art fashionistas spending on clothes and jewellery, but nothing flashy. They wore the sorts of things that only looked expensive to those who could read labels without seeing them. It was a code.

Daniel felt completely out of his league. He was far too low down the art press rankings to qualify for an invitation to this event but had been whistled up to stand in for Fay, who was under emergency orders from her personal trainer to spend a week at a health spa. Crispin Finch had been out of editorial favour since refusing to cover the Orlovsky story.

Things had to be pretty serious for FLP to miss the premier event in the British art calendar, but her trainer had apparently informed her that she was no longer as young as she had been – which, bitched Crispin, was what triggered the collapse.

In a crowd like this Daniel would normally have been invisible, but he found it parting deferentially before his crutches. It occurred to him that he should have asked for a wheelchair, as he quickly discovered that crutches and notepads don't mix. Just as well, perhaps. In this exalted company a pad would have marked him out as an outsider; better to put it away and trust to memory. More annoying was having to refuse the champagne for fear of ending up doing an Enzo.

The announcement of the winner would be made at 9pm, which gave Daniel an hour to check out the competition. He found the Tunisian artist's film surprisingly touching, especially the climactic moment of the stolen nuzzle between the veiled woman and the blinkered horse. But the other nominees' work was unremarkable. The Lithuanian made what he called reductionist abstracts, lifting the paint off in parallel lines with a squeegee, and the Taiwanese had filled a gallery with discarded circuit boards and called the installation *Copper Mountain.*

Tinker-Stone was showing two new videos. A wall panel mentioned her previous nomination for *Gutted*, "a meditation on the tragicomic mask in the context of today's popular culture, where the sports stadium has replaced the theatre as the principal locus of communal catharsis". In the first of her new videos, *Smile Please*, she "had turned her lens inward to examine her own milieu via the self-referential device of a series of 'self-portraits' reflected in the smiles of art world insiders". The second video, *Performance Art*, took a new direction. There was no accompanying explanation because, said the wall text, the artist felt that it spoke for itself.

Performance Art was a film of a painter in his studio, showing him working on a long vertical canvas. Although the film was shot from behind, the painter was instantly identifiable as an archetypal bohemian of the old school, with a pink flowered shirt and mint-green trousers – not to mention tortoiseshell-tinted hair – competing for attention with a vibrantly coloured canvas.

The film's running time was 42 minutes – the sort of length that, under normal circumstances, only a diehard video cultist would be able to sit through – but its effect on Daniel was hypnotic. There was a lilting rhythm to the artist's repeated actions, standing back, looking, applying a dab of colour, standing back again, mixing another colour, scratching the back of his neck, looking out the window, taking an occasional swig from a mug on the table. Daniel watched, oddly mesmerised, as he took a rag and removed a patch of viridian from the centre left of the canvas, reached for a tube of violet, squeezed it on the palette, reconsidered, placed a dab of dark red on the top right, thought again, took a smaller brush, loaded it with blue and drew the outline of a form – a horse? – on the bottom left.

He was not an elegant figure – in three-quarter profile you could see a beer gut – but his movements back and forth across the canvas had the grace and poise of a kind of painterly Tai Chi. And it wasn't only his movements that held the eye; the painting itself was in motion. Forms came into focus, coalesced and receded as parts of the picture were built up and scraped off. The image was in flux. With time-lapse photography, thought Daniel, it would have been like staring into a fire: a glint here, a flicker there, a deep glow, a sudden pool of darkness. The soundtrack, too, with its scuffs and scrapes and soft footfalls, lulled you into a meditative state. You could almost hear the background hum of thought, interrupted by an occasional sound of throat-clearing.

Something about that sound struck Daniel as familiar, though he couldn't put his finger on what. He was puzzling over it when an attendant came in to say that the prize announcement was about to be made in the next room. The crowd swarmed to the door and Daniel let them. He wasn't going to fight his way through on crutches when he could hear perfectly well from the comfortable seating in front of the video.

The prize envelope this year was to be opened by celebrity photographer Dario Testaccio. Daniel heard a heavily accented voice announcing: "And the winner of this year's Ars Nova Prize for ars innovation is... Tammi Tinkerston!"

As Tinker-Stone began her acceptance speech, Daniel watched the painter in her video turn away from the canvas to wipe his brush on some sheets of newspaper on the table beside him, and he suddenly realised what was familiar about him. Of course! He was the painter from the allotments. And in a gap exposed by his turning movement, Daniel noticed something else that looked familiar.

Propped on a shelf just to the right of the easel was a small canvas of a seaside scene with boats and figures in a radically different style to the one he was painting. The picture looked unfinished, but it was without a doubt the Derain of *The Harbour at Collioure* featuring on the cover of next month's *Marquette*.

On his way out Daniel asked the Head of Press if she would let him have a copy of the video, as *Marquette* would like to run a profile of the Ars Nova winner in the following issue.

Chapter XXXXIV

When the party broke up, Jeremy Gaunt went back up to his office. It was after ten but he had another hole to fill, this time in next year's exhibition schedules.

The previous summer, when it had become perfectly clear that the money to finish the building works would not be forthcoming either from government or private sources, the painful decision had been made to mothball the State Gallery extension until further notice. It had fallen to Gaunt to break the news to Orlovsky that the headline Russian exhibition planned for the launch of the new extension would have to be cancelled.

Gaunt was surprised at how badly he took it. Fair enough, the Orlovsky Gallery had put work into the show, but the dealer seemed to take it personally. Gaunt had never seen him lose his composure, let alone his legendary temper, which he was shocked to find himself on the receiving end of. Orlovsky raged about having delivered the Wise Collection into his hands, only to be rewarded by a kick in the teeth. His Russian backers, he warned – indeed almost threatened – were not used to this sort of treatment. It was the last they would be contributing to the State Gallery's newly established Russian Acquisitions Fund, or to any other funds for that matter.

He got so worked up that Gaunt worried he would have a heart attack. To calm him down, he had to promise to make space for a smaller exhibition in the main building. It wouldn't get the fanfare of the launch exhibition but it was the best he could offer in the circumstances, as he was sure Orlovsky understood. On the State Gallery's part, it would mean cancelling an exhibition that had been years in preparation.

And now, just when planning on the Russian exhibition should have been gathering pace, Orlovsky had vanished off the face of the earth. If the show failed to materialise, a three-month gap would open up in next year's autumn programme that would be almost impossible to plug. Exhibitions were complicated enough to organize without the problem of procuring loans at short notice.

Where were the institutions willing to lend to a show that was due to open in less than a year's time? Gaunt's mind was a blank, but at least here in his eerie, with the place to himself, he had the rare luxury of space to think. He relished these moments of solitude in the vast empty building. Alone in his control room on the seventh floor, he felt like the brain in the State Gallery cranium.

Tonight, admittedly, the brain was a little fogged. It wasn't alcohol. Gaunt never drank at receptions; in his position he couldn't miss a beat. No, it was cumulative exhaustion from rattling around year in year out on the hamster wheel of gallery administration – something of which he was forcibly reminded every day by the Jötnar & Rasmussen fairground wheel recently installed in the gallery atrium. Made of recycled pumpjacks supplied by sponsors Oil Britannia, the wheel had attracted environmental protests but was proving very popular with younger visitors who, with their numbers swelled by the protestors, were giving a welcome boost to attendance figures.

Gaunt's mind was not on the Danish duo, however. He was thinking about the Tammy Tinker-Stone video of that old artist pottering about in his shed. A dying breed, he'd thought while watching it, and the thought had filled him with a sense of loss he couldn't dispel.

It was that video that had won Tinker-Stone the prize. Gaunt had driven the decision through over the heads of the other judges, two of whom – led by Orlovsky's exhibitions director Tom Jonson – had been gunning for the Taiwanese circuit boards. Jonson dismissed the video as lacking in conceptual rigour; he found it whimsical, sentimental and old-fashioned. Even its kooky subtitle, 'The Way Forwards Is Backwards', was retrograde.

Apparently that was the old painter's motto. Thinking of it now, Gaunt broke into a smile, one of those secret, unforced, oddly youthful smiles that could still, on rare occasions, crack the carapace.

No possibility of the State Gallery going backwards; onwards and upwards was the only course. Nothing could be allowed to interfere with the march of artistic progress dictated by the market. Still, though a backwards move was out of the question, it occurred to Gaunt as he looked out of his window onto the building site below, half abandoned since the cranes migrated north, that a sideways move might get him out of not just one hole, but two.

It hadn't escaped the notice of his paymasters at the Department of Arts & Community Cohesion that the highest attendance figures at a contemporary art exhibition that year had been for a show of graffiti artist POG in his hometown of Plymouth. During its three-month run at the City Art Gallery POG's show had attracted 300,000 visitors from all over the country, many of whom had never been in an art gallery – a demographic to die for.

Those figures would guarantee the Plymouth show a coveted ranking in *Marquette*'s annual league table of the world's most popular art exhibitions, a list the State Gallery always struggled to get onto. Despite all the media coverage and the televised presentation, the Ars Nova audience could never come near that figure, especially not with this year's unspectacular line-up. Art critics might get off on 'conceptual rigour' but for the general public it spelled 'rigor mortis'. Well, Madani's horses should pull in the odd punter who'd wandered in for a ride on the big wheel. He wondered if Jötnar & Rasmussen could be persuaded to build a rollercoaster next year.

Plymouth, imagine. The State was prepared to lose out to the Louvre and half the public museums in Japan, where gallery-going was a national religion, but Plymouth? That was a real slap in the face. The very thought of it, in fact, was enough to shake him out of his funk.

As he watched the huge ovoid hole of the stalled extension's foundations filling with water from the November rains, an idea that could solve the Russian and the egg problems at a single stroke began to take shape in Gaunt's mind. Why not turn the site into the world's biggest skate park? Throw it open to top international graffitists from around the globe – America, Australia, Brazil, Japan – and expose POG for the provincial player he was!

With an interactive zone for local taggers and workshops run by global graffiti names, it would tick all the funding boxes: regeneration, multiculturalism, audience-creation... Meanwhile the galleries that had been reserved for the Russian exhibition could host a show of related works by graffiti masters, delivering teenage taggers into the arms of the Education Department who could then redirect them towards the permanent collection. The exhibition would be temporary but the skate-park semi-permanent, remaining in place until the rest of the funding for the extension was forthcoming – if necessary, until kingdom come. And the marvellous thing about the whole scheme was that it would cost next to nothing.

Viewed from his seventh-floor window, the housing estates of South London spread out beneath Gaunt like a carpet of LEDs pulsating with potential visitor numbers. As he gazed out over them, his peripheral vision was disturbed by a slight movement on the building site below. A gang of workmen in hard hats appeared to be digging a trench in the shadow of the construction hoarding near the site entrance.

Odd, as the site had been more or less deserted for months. At this time of night it must be emergency drainage work

– there had been worries about standing water affecting the foundations. And in fact the men were lowering a half-pipe into the trench. A half-pipe! The coincidence struck Gaunt as prophetic. For some reason the men seemed to be working in darkness, apart from the light cast by the street lamp on the other side of the hoarding. Strange that nobody had said anything about it, but minor problems were often kept from him. He sometimes suspected that he was perceived as a control freak.

He shut down his computer, switched off the office lights, took the lift down to the ground floor, bid the security guards goodnight and took the back exit to the car park serving the construction site, now deserted apart from his Toyota Prius and a builder's van.

As he got into his car he could hear the workmen on the other side of the hoarding speaking a language he didn't understand. Polish probably, though it lacked the note of complaint he associated with Polish. To his ears it sounded more like Russian.

The State should really be employing British workers; he'd speak to the architects' office in the morning. But in the morning other things intervened, and he forgot.

And so it was that Orlovsky's State burial went undiscovered.

Chapter XXXXV

Yasmin suppressed a yawn as she dumped the stack of envelopes on her desk.

Nothing interesting ever came by post these days; it was either junk mail or forms. Before the cuts there had been a secretary to sift it, but now that Yasmin had to open the mail herself she put the chore off until the end of the day to stop it taking the edge off the morning.

This evening she was running late and she'd arranged to meet her mum at the station with Sami. Since the Orlovsky case had turned into a murder inquiry – although no body had so far been found – her security detail had been moved to other duties. The advice from on high was that it was safe to bring her son home. Sami was missing his mum, and he was missing school.

The train was due into St Pancras in 40 minutes. If she prioritised, she could pick out the urgent-looking letters and leave the rest until tomorrow morning. She riffled through the stack of envelopes, pulled out a small jiffy with a Special Delivery stamp and tore it open. A CD fell out accompanied by a folded proof of the front page of November's *Marquette*.

On the CD was a Post-it note with the cryptic message: 'FF 40 mins'.

She could have left it to the next day, but it was Daniel's writing. She slipped the disk into her CD drive and fast-forwarded.

To her astonishment, she found herself watching a film of Patrick Phelan working on one of those seven canvases in his shed.

How did Daniel know about the Phelan case? She hadn't said anything. It was still under investigation.

It was a moment before she realised he didn't know. What he was drawing her attention to was a little painting of a harbour scene leaning up against the wall behind the artist – the exact same painting as was staring up at her from the front page of next month's *Marquette*. The difference was that the *Marquette* version had an antique gilt frame and had just been sold by the auction house RazzleDeVere for £16m.

The Phelan case was getting more and more interesting. Scribbling 'I'll explain tomorrow, Yasmin,' on the Post-it, she dropped the CD and proof on Burningham's desk on her way out.

Chapter XXXXVI

'£16M DERAIN A FAKE? BOUNDS GREEN ARTIST ARRESTED IN DAWN SWOOP'. A special report by *Marquette*'s Daniel Colvin appeared on page 3 of *The Times* of Friday 6ᵗʰ November.

"In the early hours of yesterday, two weeks after auctioneer RazzelDeVere's sale of Derain's 'lost' *Harbour at Collioure* for £16m broke auction records for the artist, Metropolitan police officers assisted by specialists from the Art & Antiques Unit raided a suburban semi-detached property in Bounds Green. A tip-off had led detectives to the studio of 67-year-old artist Patrick Phelan, a part-time art teacher, who was taken in for questioning on suspicion of forgery.

"A search of the artist's studio in a shed at the back of the property revealed, among a cache of unidentified paintings, what appeared to be a half-finished copy of a Modigliani nude. Police also took away photographs thought to depict missing paintings and a reference work on artists' signatures.

"The suspect was taken to Paddington Green Police Station and later released on bail.

"On the basis of evidence collected at the Bounds Green property police later visited a basement flat in Chelsea, home of the art dealer James Duval, former head of the Impressionist & Modern Art Department at RazzellDeVere. Officers were seen removing some 30 pictures from the flat, mostly land-scapes and nudes by an unidentified artist.

"Mr Duval is assisting police with their enquiries.

"In a separate development, the UK border agency has been alerted to look out for a third suspect, the interior architect Martin Phelan, son of the artist, reported to have taken delivery of a consignment of canvases from the Bounds Green address in the past few weeks. It is feared he may attempt to leave the country, if he has not already done so.

"The clients of Martin Phelan's architectural practice included many prominent figures in the London art world, among them the missing gallerist Bernard Orlovsky. This has prompted speculation that the gallerist's disappearance might be connected with an art forgery ring, though that seems unlikely. Orlovsky dealt almost exclusively in contemporary art and no evidence of contemporary forgeries has come to light."

Fay blew on the sliced ginger tea that had replaced macchiatos in her regime since the health farm visit. She was proud of Daniel, and of herself. What a find he was! The young man had a genius for investigative journalism. He was a little cagey about divulging his sources, but on his record so far she was prepared to trust him. He kept his ear to the ground. His exclusives were raising the magazine's profile, and the circulation figures were showing the effects.

Only last week she had been invited on *News.am* to discuss Orlovsky's disappearance. Her fear now was that she'd lose Daniel to a mainstream paper. But no, he was too interested in art and the mainstream press were only interested in art prices or crimes. All the same, he'd earned a promotion. Crispin Finch had lost his nose for the business. All that guff about the fake Derain on November's front page had been a huge embarrassment. It didn't help that the mainstream papers had all made the same mistake. *Marquette* should know better.

Crispin was getting past his sell-by. OK, he was younger than her but he didn't look it, with his papery skin and rheumy eyes. She was tired of his grumpy presence around the office; he was always in a pet about something these days.

Chapter XXXXVII

In an airless room on the first floor of Southwark Crown Court, Judge Levene removed his wig from its steel box and shook out its tails.

The horsehair, he noticed, was looking tired and fuzzy. It was time he acquired a new one, but not worth the investment. He would be retiring next year.

He put it on, tucked his hair inside it – at 69, he still had hair of his own – and checked that the tails weren't caught under his robe. The rush-hour tube to London Bridge had been suffocating and despite the air-conditioning in the courtroom, it was the sort of day when you sweated into your wig. But this morning's proceedings ought to be a breeze. One of the accused had pleaded guilty and the other hadn't a legal leg to stand on.

It had been an odd sort of trial. In his 10 years on the bench Levene had never seen the public gallery so full in what was not, after all, a celebrity case. It was a more colourful crowd than usual and, as far as the women in the front row went, noticeably more attractive.

A surprising turnout for two pensionable fraudsters. Wives and girlfriends? Unlikely. Artists' models? Possibly. The women certainly carried themselves well. There was one in particular, a woman of a certain age, who had something almost majestic in her bearing – the way the head sat on the neck, and the neck on the shoulders.

Married happily to the same woman for forty years, Solomon Levene did not regard himself as a judge of horseflesh, though he was something of a connoisseur of art. A dabbler given to donning a panama hat on holiday and painting watercolour landscapes for relaxation, he was a firm believer in the therapeutic benefits of art. Three years earlier, he had started the charity New Life for Lifers to bring art into prisons, a cause to which he was hoping to devote his retirement. He collected contemporary paintings in a modest way, under a self-imposed – well, wife-imposed – limit of £500. It was astonishing what you could buy for such small sums if you knew what to look for. And Levene had an eye. He could tell that the fakes at the centre of this case were extraordinarily good.

After 40 years in the law, 10 on the bench and 30 as a criminal defence barrister, Levene was looking forward to retirement. He was tired of court business and, unlike colleagues who had grown comfortably into their roles, felt increasingly uneasy as the years went by about adjudicating over other people's lives. The older he got, the more unfathomable life's mysteries appeared to him and the less qualified he seemed to be to pronounce upon them. But this case dealt with an area of life he knew something about, and he had to admit that he was rather enjoying it.

New faces in the media gallery too, he'd noticed. Arts press, presumably – not the usual crowd of jaded legal journalists. At the start of the trial, when the artist stood to enter his plea, the judge had seen a young reporter grinning as he took notes. Some of the jurors too had been suppressing smiles.

The man had certainly been unconventionally dressed. Instead of the customary dark suit for a court appearance, he was wearing a turquoise-striped gondolier's shirt with the sleeves rolled up and a pair of mirror sunglasses hooked into the neck. His bottom half was clad in maroon trousers, and Levene thought he caught a flash of canary yellow socks.

Perhaps the defendant felt that his guilty plea absolved him of the need to impress the court. His associate, who had pleaded not guilty, wore a suit. Still, there was something oddly imposing about the artist's presence. In response to the question: "Patrick Aloysius Phelan, you are charged with conspiracy to defraud: how do you plead, guilty or not guilty?" he had answered: "Guilty" in a sonorous voice. The accent was residually Irish, the tone surprisingly authoritative.

Patrick Phelan and his associate, the art dealer James Duval, had both been charged with conspiracy to defraud and the evidence against them was incontrovertible. In the artist's case, a half-finished copy of a Modigliani nude with a photo of a missing original had been retrieved from his North London studio, and a painting sold as a Derain at auction for £16m had appeared in a video of the artist at work. In the dealer's case, a police raid on his basement flat in Chelsea had revealed, hidden among a large collection of 'genuine' Phelans, three further forgeries of works by Alexei von Jawlensky, Albert Marquet and Maurice de Vlaminck. The five canvases had been key exhibits in court.

A third man – the artist's son Martin Phelan – had been wanted for questioning, but had declined the request to give evidence by video link from the Gulf State of Khaleej where he was currently resident. The set of 12 canvases that a neighbour had witnessed him removing from his father's property had not been traced. Their large size and square format argued against their being copies of early modern paintings and, in the absence of evidence to the contrary, the police had accepted the artist's explanation – corroborated by his students – that the canvases were a decorative commission for an interior design consultancy specialising in art for high-end hotels.

A fourth man, Nigel Vouvray-Jones – director of the auction house RazzleDeVere that had handled the sale of the fake Derain – had been questioned under caution and released. Although open to accusations of professional negligence, he appeared to have acted in good faith. As a former member of staff, Cassandra Pemberton – author of the auction catalogue authenticating the work as "quintessential blue-chip Fauve"

– had explained in the witness box, scientific checks were not always performed on paintings where the provenance was sound. In this case the painting had been sourced through a reliable dealer and the provenance, though unusual, had made a good story. Good stories sold pictures and an auction house that looked too closely into a painting's history risked discovering things it would rather not know. In the art business, uncovering fakes was to no one's benefit; ignorance was bliss for all concerned.

Ms Pemberton had since left the company.

Tests on the paintings conducted by independent experts from Westerby's and conservators at the Courtauld had revealed that, of the three completed copies, two were painted over previous images and the third – the Vlaminck – was on a form of undyed linen employed by Habitat in the 1970s for its popular design of Director's Chair. Radiographic analysis of the Jawlensky revealed an earlier painting of a kitten playing with a ball of wool, signed Dorothy Paton and dated 1963, on a standard grade mountboard marketed by Sanders & Peyton under the brand name 'Girtin' in the post-war period. But X-radiography of the Derain picture connected it directly to Phelan, revealing barges on a river, possibly the Thames, with the letters PP inscribed in the bottom right-hand corner in the Roman serifed capitals typical of the artist's signature. Examination of the large number of other signature works by Phelan in Duval's possession demonstrated beyond reasonable doubt that the over-painted image was his. A similar river scene with barges bearing the same signature had appeared in evidence alongside an X-radiograph of the Derain.

The artist's involvement in forgery was beyond dispute, but the dealer had continued to protest his innocence. His defence was that Phelan had approached him with the pictures, claiming to have come across them among a stack of antique frames in a junk shop in Paris. If Duval hadn't looked at the pictures too closely, it was because he felt that was the auction house's job. After his researches into the paintings' provenance had traced them back to the Meyer Collection, his only deception had been to embellish the truth by constructing a convincing back-story, one that an auction house would be likely to swallow. Having once headed a department at RazzelDeVere, he knew exactly what sort of story that was.

He felt no guilt about misleading a firm that had unfairly dismissed him. What he felt guilty about was the paltry fee he had paid Phelan for a painting that would later realise £16m. But the fee was all he could afford at the time, as he was in the throes of an expensive divorce. He'd had every intention of making reparation after the sale of the work.

Duval's counsel, in closing arguments for the defence, assured the jury that his client was a man of previous good character and sound professional reputation. In the 30 years he had worked at fine art auctioneers RazzellDeVere as the firm's expert in modern European art, he had become an acknowledged authority in his field.

Unfortunately, in the current state of the market, auction houses no longer required expertise of this sort. In fact, such expertise had become an obstruction. Subjecting pictures and provenances to proper evaluation was a time-consuming and costly business that slowed the sales cycle and carried the inherent risk that the brakes might have to be applied. In today's fast-moving global market, expertise was only of academic value; in practical terms it was a liability. What was needed for the new breed of international collector with no knowledge of western art and no time to acquire any was the appearance of expertise, and that was supplied by auction sales catalogues. This was the reason Duval's employers had made him redundant, precipitating the financial and domestic crisis that had driven an honest man to deception.

In the witness box the previous week Duval had taken the unorthodox step of launching a vigorous defence of his associate, arguing that in a market denuded of professionals, artists like Phelan were the last remaining experts on painting technique. In fact, he maintained, they would soon be the only people left with the time, the motivation and visual skills to investigate how historic paintings were made. A market in which artists were the only art experts was a market wide open to abuse, especially given that, of all the contributors to the art economy, artists were the most badly paid. A recent survey had revealed that fine artists in Britain earned under £10,000pa on average from their art, out of which they had to pay for expensive materials. If an artist couldn't earn a living wage from his own art, an obvious solution was to earn it from somebody else's.

"You've seen the so-called 'fakes'," he told the court, "they're good paintings. I've not seen better, and I've seen worse by these same artists. Take *The Harbour at Collioure*. Eight months ago it was worth £16m and now it's worth nothing. If nobody knew it was a Phelan and not a Derain, it would be hanging on the wall of a museum where generations of visitors could enjoy it and art students learn from it. What does it mean to say that a picture is worth £16m? What does that monetary value measure? Nothing has materially changed in *The Harbour at Collioure* between now and when the auctioneer's hammer came down last October. It's the same painting. Even if the money were simply an investment in Derain futures it would be a safer place to put it than a Ponzi scheme, because the 'fraud' need never have come to light. Hundreds, even thousands of brilliant forgeries are hanging at this very moment on the walls of major galleries."

Levene had overruled the prosecuting counsel's objection that Duval was digressing. He had been keen to hear the dealer out, and he wasn't alone. Throughout his evidence you could have heard a paperclip drop. In the media gallery the reporters bent over their notepads scribbling; in the front row of the public gallery the women leant over the railing, displaying their décolletages to advantage. The dealer was clearly enjoying his moment, and he wasn't finished yet.

"For nearly a year my stockroom has been stuffed with paintings with this artist's signature, the double 'PP' you've seen on his 'autograph' pictures. The pictures are of subjects similar to the 'fakes' he is accused of painting – river scenes, still lifes with flowers, nudes – all painted in a signature style, the style of the artist. He has spent a lifetime developing that signature style, a style that only a top class faker would be able to copy, but the signature is worthless because it is not a recognised name. If I put the lot on the market tomorrow I'd be lucky to raise a few thousand pounds. That's the price of a lifetime's work in today's art market."

A murmur of appreciation ran through the public gallery before Levene allowed a second objection from the prosecution to stand, and the dealer was led back to the dock. He had had his say.

That was a week ago. This morning the judge would give his summing up and the jury would withdraw to consider their verdicts. He didn't expect them to take long. After the verdict was delivered, defending counsel would have the chance to put forward mitigation.

Phelan, who was representing himself, had appointed a McKenzie friend to advise him. The fact that the man was a former solicitor was unlikely to affect the sentence. Whatever the rights and wrongs of the case, the law was clear.

* * * * * * *

Southwark Crown Court looked more like a bunker to Daniel than a seat of justice. At 9.30 on a Tuesday morning the place was buzzing, with the queue for security checks stretching to the street. A young woman reporter from the *Evening Standard* explained the procedure: empty pockets – keys, phone, pen, pad, money – at the security gate and cross to the unmanned reception desk to the right of the lobby to consult the printed list of cases being heard that day.

When Daniel reached the desk, a young black kid was riffling through the list. "That's me," he announced with pride, finding his name among the defendants on trial in Court No. 13.

Daniel was taken aback. He'd somehow expected those on trial to arrive through a different entrance from the general public, but apparently the Manichean binary didn't operate in the lobby where innocence and guilt remained grey areas. It kicked in on the other side of the courtroom doors.

The trial of Patrick Aloysius Phelan and James Gerald Duval was in Court No. 2.

The lift disgorged Daniel onto a long wide corridor full of barristers in wigs and gowns, walking back and forth with bundles of papers under their arms or holding whispered conversations with their clients on the benches along the walls. Above the benches were framed reproductions of wishy-washy watercolours of flowers and fruit, the sort of anaesthetic art you'd expect to find in a dentist's waiting room.

It was Daniel's first visit to a law court. Pushing open the swing doors into Courtroom No. 2 felt like entering an ethical decompression chamber: outside, the familiar messy world of moral uncertainty; inside, an alternative universe of forensic certitude.

From his seat in the second row of the media gallery, Daniel found himself surveying the two men in the dock from the point of view of a court illustrator. The overlapping profiles gave him a reassuring sense of déjà vu. There was no illustrator in court today – the case wasn't high-profile enough for the profile treatment – but the contrast offered by the overlaid silhouettes was a missed opportunity, he thought, for a caricaturist. Between the crisp lines of Duval's chiseled nose and chin jutting smartly over the collar of his laundered shirt and the shapeless scrawl of Phelan's bulbous proboscis and dimpled jowls sinking into the sagging neck of his purple T-shirt, a latter-day Leonardo would have had a field day.

The judge would have made an interesting study too, though more for an artist of Gillray's era. Unusually, his features perfectly fitted his wig. He was an 18th century figure, small, wiry, birdlike, with sharp disconcertingly pale blue eyes. Daniel suspected that under his judicial robes he might, in silk stockings and buckled shoes, have displayed a finely turned calf.

As he got out his notepad, Daniel became aware of another pair of eyes fastened on him, as pale as the judge's but more rheumy. The new editor of RDV magazine was sitting three along from him, behind the reporter from the *Evening Standard*.

Crispin Finch would have his work cut out reversing the damage to RDV's reputation from Cassandra Pemberton's widely reported outburst in court. It would have been difficult to imagine him looking tighter-lipped than in his dying days at *Marquette*, but he was looking it now. Daniel felt a twinge of pity for his predecessor. Hard enough to lose your job of 30 years to a greenhorn with no experience who didn't really want it, worse to trade the peppery but warm-blooded FLP for the bloodless, notoriously cruel NVJ.

As the judge prepared to begin his summing up, Daniel noticed a slight disturbance in the public gallery opposite. An elderly lady in a lilac straw hat had arrived late to find all the seats taken and a swarthy, burly man stood up to offer her his place. She smiled her thanks and sat down quickly, removing the hat and putting it in her lap.

Daniel recognised the lady painter from the allotments. She seemed to have brought half the garden with her: the brim of her hat was a cornucopia of flowers.

The court fell silent as the judge began to speak.

"Ladies and gentlemen of the jury, you have heard the evidence in this case. Whilst the personal circumstances described earlier in court may have aroused some sympathy among you in offering an explanation of the accused's motivation for committing the offences, this does not lessen the gravity of the offences in the eyes of the law. You are adjudicating on a case of fraud and the task before you as a jury is simply to decide, on the evidence before you, whether the man you see before you is guilty of committing the fraudulent acts of which he stands accused.

"In a case such as this involving a high degree of skill and ingenuity, there is a risk that the very cleverness of the deception may be a factor in favorably influencing a jury's decision. But one can never condone the practice of fraud by making a false representation, and there should be no doubt in your minds that passing off an article for sale as something other than it is *is* wilful deception. We are talking here about a very large sum of money, such as most of us would not expect to earn in a lifetime. If the offences described were indeed committed by the accused, then they amount to deception on a grand scale."

It took the jury less than an hour to reach a unanimous verdict of guilty on the various counts of which James Duval was accused, although Daniel thought he detected a trace of regret in the forewoman's voice as she delivered it.

A ripple of unrest passed through the public gallery as the judge declared the morning session closed. The lady with the lilac hat pulled out a lace-trimmed hanky; the swarthy man standing at the back wiped his brow on his sleeve. The court would reconvene for sentencing after lunch.

* * * * * * * *

At 2pm everyone was back in their places, if they had ever left them. The tension in the public gallery visibly tightened as Patrick Phelan was asked if he wished to put forward mitigation before sentencing. He nodded, and after a murmured consultation with the man beside him stood up a little unsteadily and was led from the dock by an usher. In the witness box he pulled a crumpled sheet of notes from the cargo pocket of his shorts and smoothed it carefully out on the lectern in front of him. He spread his hands, which were quivering slightly, and cleared his throat.

"My friend Dino over there," he nodded towards the public gallery, "who is an architect, by the way, not a lawyer, tells me that where he comes from they have a proverb: 'The man who defends himself has a fool for a lawyer'. Well, I'm a fool, always have been. If I wasn't I'd never have gone into this rum business called art. But I can't see the point in hiring a lawyer to waste hours of everyone's time saying what I can say myself in five minutes. So here goes.

"An artist's life is a struggle, and mine has been no exception. I struggled to keep my wife – lost her – and my son Marty, doing night jobs and bits of teaching to earn a crust. In the early days I had a couple of sell-out exhibitions and some mentions in the press as up-and-coming, but after coming up, if I ever did – no one told me – my career 'plateaued', as I think the expression is.

"In the past fifty years I've painted a few thousand pictures and in a good year sold a dozen, through open exhibitions, competitions, studio shows, that sort of thing. Without a gallery to represent you, those are your options. The most I've earned from a single painting, after deducting the commission, is £900.

"I don't paint pictures simply for my own pleasure, I paint them to go out in the world and spread themselves around. But of course it's also an addictive habit: 'Never a day without a line,' as the poet said. I've painted subjects I knew would never sell just because they were crying out to be painted. Unprofessional, I grant you, and no way to make a living.

"Since this is a court of law, I'll make a confession. I don't regard the daubs you've seen as a crime, nor do I regret the time I wasted on them, although they did take me away from my life's work. As Picasso freely admitted, all artists are thieves – the good ones, anyway. We learn our trade by copying other artists and stealing their best licks. Even later in life, when we're wizened old pros, it can be a useful exercise to return to the practice.

"The only copy I regret, for a number of reasons, is the Modigliani." A nervous glance towards the public gallery drew a smile from a pretty young woman in the front row, who shook her head disparagingly, jiggling her earrings. "That was inexcusable and gratuitous – I did it for the money. I'd nothing to learn from the Eyetie's sloppy drawing.

Sorry Dino, no reflection on your countrymen," he picked out the swarthy man standing with his arms folded at the back, "but it's not good enough for the nation of Michelangelo.

"The other copies I'm reasonably pleased with, especially the Jawlensky. I like to think the old Ruskie would have approved. That was just the warm-up exercise needed for my final assault on my life's work, which is now completed thanks to the pressure of this prosecution. For that I'm grateful to the Crown," he addressed the judge. "There's nothing like an extended period of bail to focus the mind and sharpen the perceptions.

"One final thing. If I'd known what that Derain would sell for I'd never have painted it. No painting by any artist, dead or alive, is worth that sort of money. That is the only crime I'm ashamed of, the crime of colluding with an art market that has no understanding of the value of art."

As Phelan pulled out a red paisley handkerchief to blow his nose the public gallery erupted into applause and, in defiance of the judge's cries of 'Order!', a rose sailed through the air and landed at his feet. In the second row of the public gallery the allotment lady was standing holding her hat. For a frail old woman, she was a surprisingly good shot. Seeing an usher moving in to eject her from the court, Daniel pushed past the other reporters and out of the courtroom in time to catch her being escorted down the corridor.

At the lifts she dusted herself off and adjusted her hair. The sheepish-looking usher handed her the hat and was rewarded with a smile that deepened his embarrassment.

"Excuse me," Daniel butted in, "you're a friend of Patrick Phelan's aren't you?'

"Yes," she replied tentatively, wondering how he knew.

Daniel scribbled his address on a page of his pad and tore it off.

"If you see him, could you ask him to get in touch with me? There's a painting of his I'd like to buy."

Chapter XXXXVIII

'L-O-V-E' read the fingers holding the brush; 'H-A-T-E' read the fingers holding the palette. With intense concentration a prisoner was adding the finishing touches to his entry for the Levene Awards.

Before being banged up, none of the men in Mantonville Rec Room would have had anything to do with art other than nick it. Ponce about with a paintbrush? You had to be joking. No money in it, and no respect.

Inside was different. People accustomed to active lives – carjacking, ram-raiding, safe-blowing, assault and battery – could go stir crazy cooped up in a cell 24/7. Blokes signed up for classes out of desperation. You'd get hard nuts volunteering for 'drama therapy' or 'creative writing'. Posh birds with accents off of the BBC telling you to "act out your personal problems and negative feelings".

"Alright, darling. How long have you got?"

This was different, this was doing something with your hands. Nothing as constructive as cracking a cashpoint, but still something. There was an end product that wasn't there at the beginning. Plus if you got selected for the Levene Awards your work got shown in a public exhibition. Your painting got out on licence even if you didn't.

Best thing about the art class, though, was the teacher was an inmate, doing time for fraud. Faking pictures. The guy was crazy, Irish, off another planet but basically a geezer and bloody brilliant. He must have been because the picture he faked sold for 16 million quid and would be hanging in a fucking museum if he hadn't been rumbled. Respect.

There was none of that personal problem shite with him, he just shoved something in front of you and told you to paint it, for better or worse – preferably for worse, as he said that generally turned out better. Some of the stuff he came out with was bonkers. Last week the class was sat here painting this scissor jack with a bunch of plastic grapes and a statue of a naked woman – still life for lifers he called it – when he said he'd rather do life with a *real* naked woman and – get this – that he'd applied to the guv'nor for permission and the guv'nor had said no. Told you he was crazy. So then he says the only alternative is for one of us to strip off, like studio assistants used to do for Michelangelo or Raphael or one of them Italian Renaissance ninjas, and the rest of us to draw in the tits from imagination. The answer to that, obviously, was no too.

Pull the other one, mate, it's got knockers on.

So there we were at 3pm on a Thursday afternoon when we could have been watching the snooker, sleeves rolled up, painting plastic grapes like our lives depended on it with him stood over us like an Irish Leonardo dishing out advice. "Gently does it, you've got all the time in the world. You're *doing* time, remember? Hold your brush like this, like you're turning a key in a lock. Not breaking and entering, no – you *own* the place. Everything in the picture belongs to you, but if you burst in on it too suddenly it'll scarper."

Nuts, like I said. When he wasn't standing over you, you had to watch him or next thing you knew he'd be painting your portrait. Done Jake's the week before last, caught him in action with a look on his face like he's painting the Mona Lisa. In actual fact it was a bag of spuds and a cheese-grater and Jake's picture looked like a pile of sick and a bucket, but he got the little bastard down pat. Spitting image. His chin was green, his nose was purple and his hair was blue, but his missus, when she saw a photo, said it looked more like Jake than Jake did.

Funny thing is, at the beginning his colours looked daft but after a while they sort of grew on you. On a sunny day you'd catch yourself looking at the shadows of the bars on the cell wall and wondering what colour they really were. Before you'd have just said grey and left it at that but now you'd stare at the blimming things for hours just thinking about it. Though if anyone asked you what colours they actually were you wouldn't have a bleeding clue.

The other week Lynton was painting these oranges blue and Paddy was stood behind watching him.

"That's an interesting shade you've chosen," he says.

"Yes," says Lynton, "it goes with the maroon bananas. You know what? I'm beginning to see what you mean about colours talking to you."

"You've been spending too much time alone mate," says Jake. "What are they saying?"

"Fuck off," says Lynton.

We'll miss the old nutter now they've moved him to an open prison.

Chapter XXXXIX

Rain was falling in sheets: nice weather for ducks, crap weather for skateboarders. But one hardened individual was aquaplaning down a ramp in the StateSkate park, the cord of his anorak hood pulled tight around his nose, his sleeves pulled down over his fists like an amputee.

Look ma, no hands.

Dry in Zubarrah, thought Jeremy Gaunt as he watched the water level rising in the skate park's troughs, and the ghost of a smile momentarily troubled his face.

Who would have guessed that Martin Phelan, of all people, would turn out to be a knight in shining armour? Thank God and his old-fashioned upbringing that he'd never been rude to him. *Noblesse oblige*, his father had taught him, for a very good reason – you never knew who might come in useful one day.

MoMAK, Khaleej's new museum of modern art, was taking the Wise Collection off his hands, all bar a few plum pieces the State was hanging onto. And next year the Khaleeji Royal Family would be sponsoring an Arab Art Spring at State Gallery, all expenses paid: catalogue, installation, reception, security, the works.

In the meantime there was the Ernst van Diem exhibition, dirt cheap to mount, as it was mostly 'collection of the artist'. Since Westerby's bought out the Orlovsky galleries they had taken Ernst on, and he was acquiring quite a reputation. Every dog has his day. In a slower economy the market was warming to late developers, artists with a more considered vision. While Cosmas Byrne's dot paintings were losing their fizz, van Diem's vibrant canvases were hitting the colour spot with collectors. His naïve daubs in the style of Karel Appel were being touted as Dutch Neo-Expressionism. Needless to say the success of his former assistant had got right up what remained of Boegemann's septum, but there was nothing to be done. Since the disastrous failure of his RDV auction the dismal Dutchman's prices had collapsed, and now no one would touch him.

Gaunt noticed that the rain collecting in the troughs had formed a moat around a tumulus-shaped hump at the edge of the skate circuit near the gate to the car park. He followed the figure of the sodden skateboarder as he looped a couple of laps around it, scooted backwards, built up speed and flew over the top, landing with a swoosh of spray on the other side.

Chapter L

Duval watched the ducks diving in the prison pond. There was something reassuring, he'd discovered, about hitting rock bottom. Divorced, a convicted fraudster and a bankrupt: when he got out, it could only be a fresh start.

They'd given him three years, meaning two with good behaviour, and after one they'd moved him to Bridge Open Prison. He'd be out in four months, and thanks to Martin, he had his future mapped out.

How wrong you could be. The sale of the Degas that he'd assumed would be a disaster had been a godsend. It was the Derain that had got him arrested, while the Degas was now sitting pretty on the walls of the National Museum of Khaleej and Martin had been generous enough to save him a share. Generosity seemed to run in that family. He was still astonished by Patrick Phelan's altruism in taking the rap for his son. Would he have been that generous in his position? He couldn't say, he'd never had children.

Thank Christ he too had had the sense not to finger Martin, for entirely selfish reasons admittedly – he'd been desperate to keep the loudmouth out of court. Well, he'd learned a lesson: never underestimate a con artist. A Martin with a clean record had turned out to be of infinitely greater use than a Martin without. Without the Degas sale he could never have passed himself off as an art world mover and shaker in Khaleej. And without his, Duval's, art expertise and contacts, he would never be able to maintain that position.

When he got out, Martin was putting him on commission to source Impressionist and Modern pictures for the new museum, money no object. Since shelling out $100m at auction for a Warhol *Car Crash* at Westerby's New York, the Khaleeji Royal Family had decided to make future acquisitions by private treaty. Arabs liked to keep their dealings personal, and there's no one quite like a con man for the personal touch.

As long as Martin stayed away from architecture. Rain wasn't a problem in the Gulf, but islands can sink.

Chapter LI

In his only suit, Dr Daniel Colvin waited under the Strand entrance to Somerset House for the rain to stop. It was pissing down, he hadn't brought a coat and the number 4 bus stop for Finsbury Park was a hundred yards away in the Aldwych.

Having just been awarded a PhD from the Courtauld for his thesis on Sheddism Daniel ought by rights to have been walking on air, but the pavement was one big puddle and his shoes leaked. After two minutes of watching the steady precipitation he got tired of waiting and decided to run for it. For some strange reason, though, when he stepped out from under the archway he remained dry.

The large black umbrella over his head seemed to explain it.

"Dr Colvin?"

The voice behind him made him jump.

"I meant to surprise you, though not like that," said Yasmin, shaking raindrops off her curls. "I got off early but not quite early enough. Sorry to miss the ceremony. How did it go?"

"Pretty well, actually. Nobody laughed."

She dropped the umbrella to hug him, soaking them both.

"Come on, I'll buy you a drink. Where's good around here? I know! The Waldorf Astoria."

"You're crazy! They'll never let us in."

"Of course they will, with you in that suit." She pushed her glasses down her nose appraisingly. "You scrub up well. Plus

I've got something to celebrate too. You know that picture you reproduced in your Indian supplement? A gallery in Mumbai saw it and they want to represent me."

"That's fantastic news!" It was his turn to hug her. "The drinks are on me."

The upside-down umbrella was collecting water.

"If we get any wetter," she said, "they won't let us in."

He picked up the umbrella and shook out the water as he steered her purposefully towards the kerb.

"Watch out!" she shouted as they narrowly missed a cab that was pulling out after dropping off a fare. "You know what they say in India? A doctor is only a doctor when he has killed one or two patients. But you don't have to take it literally, Dr Colvin. It's only a proverb."

Chapter LII

"Nice stamp," said the female warder, handing Pat a letter. "Where's that from then?"

The design showed a falcon hovering over a pearl-shaped island, the falcon red, the island silver, the sea blue.

"I don't know," said Pat, extracting the contents. He didn't recognise the stamp but he knew the writing. That childish, unformed script could only be Marty.

He pulled out a sheet of paper folded in four and, with a slight tremor in his fingers, opened it. The words 'Desert Pearl Royal Residence and Spa, Khaleej' were embossed in gold capitals along the top.

"Dear Dad,

Apologies for not getting in touch sooner. As you know, letter writing's not my strong point and since arriving in this earthly paradise I've been run off my feet.

I hope they've been treating you alright in chokey. You're a dad in a million – I'll never forget what you've done for me. Unfortunately what with one thing and another I can't be there to meet you when you get out, but you must fly straight out here – I'll send you the ticket.

This place is brilliant. Sun, sea and sand – not your usual subjects, I admit, but you always seem to find something to paint. A pair of the Cat's Pajamas the barman mixes and, I promise you, everything looks rosy. The weather's fantastic, it never rains. The desalinated water tastes like piss, but who waters their whiskey?

To get down to business. I've been in touch with James in Bridge Open Prison and he's agreed to represent you. There's been a lot of interest in your work – you're a famous painter now Dad – and James is planning a retrospective when he gets out.

But here's the big news now, listen to this. A month ago Her Highness Sheika Fatima, the third wife of the Emir in charge of this paradise isle, went to Houston and saw the Rothko Chapel and came back wanting something similar here. She started complaining that the Pearl Island development is soul-less – she was educated in Paris – and she's decided a secular chapel is what's needed. Her idea was that non-Muslim foreign tourists could use the place to recharge their spiritual batteries, and with a central location in the Oasis Mall the locals could also use it as a chill-out space while shopping.

She wanted big paintings like the Rothkos but less abstract, with more stuff going on people could tune into, and she asked if I could recommend an artist. Well of course Dad I immediately thought of you. I rang Dino and told him to go to The Shed and take some pictures of The Seven Seals. She's seen them, loves them, she's over the moon. All we're waiting for is the nod from you to ship the pictures over and we can get on with designing the building. I'm working with a team of international starchitects, so no worries.

Fan-bloody-tastic or what?

I enclose a plan of the design so far."

Love

Marty

PS. You're the best dad in the world.

PPS. I had to change the title for religious reasons, hope you don't mind.

Pat's hands were shaking as he felt in the envelope and pulled out two folded sheet of tracing paper. One was a ground plan of a chapel-shaped space with a seven-sided apse at one end; the other was an elevation of the apse, with the Seals in place.

A lump formed in Pat's throat. It was all he'd dreamed of.

"Chapel of Contemplation", read the caption, "with Patrick Phelan's 'The Seven Heavens' installed.'

Seven Heavens? What the hell!

Any reservations Pat felt were swept away in a breaking wave of parental affection.

Marty had done him proud. Blood was thicker than water. Seven seals, seven heavens, what was the difference? Meaning lay in the eye of the beholder. What mattered was that the paintings had a home. And what a home it would be! An Arabian palace.

"Good news?" The warder was watching him with interest. "You look like you've died and gone to heaven."

Pat jumped. He'd forgotten she was there.

Not a bad looking woman, actually – good strong features in a pleasant-shaped face.

"My dear, you don't know how right you are."

He stuffed the plans back into the envelope and before she could stop him he had grabbed the warder round the waist and was waltzing her around the mail-room cheek-to-cheek singing 'Heaven, I'm in heaven…" in a fruity baritone.

"What on earth are you doing?" yelped the warder, who was too young to know the Irving Berlin classic.

"I'm not on earth," sang Pat, "I'm in heaven… heaven, and my heart beats so that I can hardly speak…"

"Let me go before I have you put in solitary," she struggled to say, but she was laughing too hard to get the words out.

Pat felt the laughter shake her diaphragm through her uniform. Nice body, on the chunky side but firm. Surprisingly small waist over spreading hips.

He wondered if she'd pose for him. Never hurt to ask.

Lightning Source UK Ltd.
Milton Keynes UK
UKOW04f0847051217
313900UK00001B/124/P